THE [illegible] ST OF STONEHENGE

By

Raymond Warrillow

ISBN 978-1-909435-88-9

THE HIGH PRIEST OF STONEHENGE

It is 2200 BC in England

Chapter One

Ord opened his eyes. The light of dawn was filtering into his hut. He climbed from under his sleeping skins, picked up his armour, his bow and his quiver and walked out of his hut. Dip, his pet dog, who always slept with him, followed him. His father, Serdin, who was the leader of the tribe, had several dogs who guarded the animals and the village, but Dip was Ord's dog, and he followed Ord everywhere. Ord shared his hut with five of his brothers and two of his sisters. Two of his older sisters and two of his older brothers were now married and had their own huts, and his youngest sister, who was still being breastfed, slept in Serdin's hut.

Ord walked over to the cesspit that he had helped dig, gripped the rope and sat on the pole that had been placed across the cesspit so that you had something to sit on when you defecated. The rope was to prevent people from falling in. He was seventeen, had a full beard and was one of the tallest and strongest men in the village.

He defecated, wiped his backside on some grass and walked over to Ess. She was sitting outside Serdin's hut, breastfeeding her newborn baby girl. Ess was the latest of Serdin's three wives. Ord's mother had died a long time ago.

"What are you going to call her, Ess?" he asked. Names did not always have a meaning; they were sometimes just sounds to distinguish one person from another.

"I don't know," she said. Ess was a sad person who rarely smiled and looked older than her twenty years. "You think of a name that no one else uses."

Ord sat down, stroked Dip and tried to think of a new name. "What about Nuss? No one else is called Nuss."

"It's too much like my name," she said. "We would get confused."

He blew out his cheeks. "I know. Mell. Let's call her Mell."

"Mell it is," she said. "I wonder if she'll live?"

"I hope so," he said. "How many babies have you had?"

"Three with my first husband, but they all died, and then my husband died. I'm no good at having babies."

"It doesn't matter," he said. "Serdin has two other wives and has eight sons and five daughters."

"I'd still like to have my own children," she said. "I'd like a son. Sons are very important, especially to the leader of a tribe."

Ord sat thinking about the land and the people who lived in it. His tribe of over three thousand five hundred people lived in fifteen villages spread over a great distance. Each village built their huts in the centre of the land it owned. Most of the villages in his tribe had at least ten huts, and some had as many as thirty. His village was in the centre of the tribe. It was the largest and most important of all the villages. It contained forty-five huts. Most huts were round, had a wooden frame, walls covered in mud and dung and a roof covered in thatch. Serdin lived in a very large, oblong hut. There were hundreds of tribes in his land. Each tribe had a leader who lived in the centre of his land and who made all the major decisions. The leader of a tribe was a very powerful man, and what he said was law. Each tribe also had a holy man, who was also a very powerful man. Their holy man was called Morteen.

According to the old wise men in his village, the tribes used to fight each other over land rights. The leaders in the land had now agreed on who owned the land, and they had set up boundary markers around the land of each tribe. The tribes no longer fought each other, but raiding parties sometimes attacked his village and other villages in his tribe and tried to take their animals and possessions. For this reason, the animals were always guarded. Ord's job, along with two other men, was to guard the village animals when they were grazing.

Ord put on his armour that he wore over his everyday clothes. His everyday clothes, which he always slept in, even during the summer, consisted of a tunic, trousers made from soft animal skins and shoes made of stiff hide. Ord's armour consisted of a triple layer of thick hide from wild cattle that would stop an arrow. The other men in the tribe and the two men who guarded the animals did not wear armour. They said that it was too heavy to carry. Ord always wore his triple-layered armour, even during the summer when it was hot.

A few years ago, a neighbouring village in his tribe had been attacked by raiders. The raiders killed the three men guarding the animals and took their animals. And even though the animals were branded, they were never found. The raiders ambushed the men by creeping up on them and shooting them in the back. Each of the men had died from their wounds. Very few men survived after being shot in the body by an arrow.

"Will you get me a beaker of water?" Ess asked. "The baby needs washing. I'm sure more comes out of this baby than goes in."

Ord picked up a beaker and walked to the stream, followed by Dip.

He had a very good life and always had food to eat and beer to drink. Serdin owned most of the animals in the village and was a very wealthy man. He had rings, a bracelet and a necklace made of gold. Each village had a brewer, a medicine man, a flint knife maker, a potter, a baker, a basket maker, a tailor, a bow maker, farmers and miners. Some also had boat builders and workers in metal.

Beer was very important, and a special hut had been built by Erd, the brewer, for brewing. Many other men had tried to brew beer, but their beer had not tasted as good as Erd's did. Erd claimed it was because he put a secret ingredient into his beer. All the adults drank alcoholic drinks every day if they could afford it.

Ord knelt down by the stream and filled the beaker with water. When he was a child, he had dreamed that when he grew up, he would be given the job of being one of the stone shapers or one of the men who moved the huge stones that were used in large temple buildings in honour of the gods. Instead, he had been given the job of guarding the animals. He was disappointed, although it was better than being a miner. He would hate to have to go deep under the ground to mine flint, copper, gold, silver and tin.

Ord took the water back to Ess and then returned to his hut to wake up his brothers. "Come on, you lot," Ord said. "It's time to get up. There's work to be done."

"The sun's still sleeping," Dain, who was thirteen, said.

"Just get up, Dain," Ord said. "I'm leaving you in charge. Make sure the birds and the pigs are fed. And make sure you fix the fence around the birds."

Dain stood up. He was now almost as tall as Ord. "I will." He grinned. "And you make sure that the animals are not stolen."

"I always do," Ord said.

Ord walked over to where the animals were penned in, sat on the fence and waited for the other two guards to arrive. He watched his brother Arn, who was six, begin to feed the birds, ducks, chickens and geese with grain. The ducks and the geese ate grass, but the grain helped to fatten them up. They had their wings clipped and so did not fly away. Birds were very tasty. The villagers also ate swans and other birds that floated on the lakes. These water birds could not be domesticated. If you clipped the wings of a swan and put it in with the other birds, it would fight them.

Ord's brother Arn walked up to him. "I want to be a bowman like you, Ord." He picked up Ord's bow, which was as long as a man was tall and examined it. "What do you have to do to be a good bowman?"

"You need to be tall and very strong," Ord said. "Only a few men are tall enough and strong enough to be a good bowman."

"They say that you're the best shot in the village," Arn said. "They say that you can hit a rabbit at a hundred paces."

"You need to be nearer than that to hit a rabbit," Ord said.

"How do you become a good shot?" Arn asked.

"You need to practice."

"Do you practice?"

"Yes. I practice every day. Aren't you supposed to be lighting the fire? They'll be wanting to cook breakfast soon."

Arn put the bow down. "I suppose so. I hate lighting fires." He walked off towards where they cooked the food.

The sun began to rise over the trees. There were very few clouds in the sky, and it looked as if it was going to be a warm, sunny day. The other two guards arrived. They released the animals from the pens and began to drive them towards the grazing land. The other two guards were brothers and did not have the brains of a chicken. Their two dogs and Dip did most of the work in driving the animals to where the grass was the longest. When the animals were in the right position, the two brothers and Ord separated to form a large circle around the animals to protect them from raiders.

Ord positioned himself on a high ridge of ground that gave him a panoramic view for several miles, and he would be able to see any approaching raiders. He would also be able to keep an eye on the two brothers. He did not trust them. They were lazy and spent most of the day sleeping. While periodically keeping an eye out for raiders, he practised hitting a tree with his arrows until his arm ached. He used the flint knife he always carried to dig the flint arrowheads out of the tree trunk. He was now an expert with a bow and knew all there was to know about warfare.

It was very difficult to shoot a man with a bow if he was looking at you and was more than sixty paces from you. If you tried, he would see the arrow and step out of its way. It would be a waste of an arrow. If the man was thirty paces or less from you, it would be impossible for him to step out of the way of the arrow. The reason why Ord always wore his armour was because nearly all the men who were killed by an arrow were shot in the back. Some men said, before they died, that they did not see the man with the bow who shot them. Their land was full of bushes and trees that could conceal a raider.

When Ord first began practising with the bow and shooting at a tree as wide as a man's body from thirty paces, he had only one hit in twenty shots. He now hit the tree with every shot. He was probably the best archer in the village. The untreated hide that he used as armour, which just covered the trunk of the body, was very thick and stiff and came from wild cattle. The hide from domesticated cattle was not quite thick enough. Wild cattle were twice as large as domesticated cattle. When testing his armour, he found that sometimes an arrow would go through two layers of hide but not through three layers. And even though the point of the arrowhead might sometimes go through three layers of hide and would cut into the flesh, the arrowhead would be prevented from going into the flesh of the body.

He smiled when he saw his eight-year-old sister, Helm, bringing him his food. She was always singing, and he often heard her before he saw her.

"Hurry up," he shouted. "I'm starving."

"I'm going as fast as I can," she said. "This basket is very heavy." She walked up to him, handed him the wicker basket containing the food, and began to stroke Dip. "I always come to you first before the two brothers so that you can pick the best food."

"I know, which is why I love you so much, Helm," he said. He looked into the basket. "Oh, no."

"What's wrong?" she asked.

"The baker's burnt the bread again." He picked up the least burnt loaf. "I bet he was drunk."

"He's always drunk," she said. "Is the chicken all right?"

He picked up the largest piece of chicken and took a bite. "Yes. The chicken's fine."

"I've also bought you some beer," she said, "but don't tell the brothers. Jugs of beer are very heavy to carry, and I would have to make two journeys if I took them beer."

He took the jug of beer out of the basket and put it on the ground. He would drink it later. The two brothers were watching him, and he did not want them to know that Helm had bought him beer. "I never talk to the two brothers. They're raving mad."

"I know they are," she said. "They always say the same thing to me when I take them their food."

"And what's that?"

"They both want to marry me."

"They can't both marry you," he said. "And they can't choose a wife until they've built a hut."

"They always say that they intend to choose me as their wife when they've built their huts. They also ask me to choose which one of them I would like to marry."

"And what do you say?"

"I always tell them that I don't want to marry either of them. I know that when a man has built a hut and chooses a woman to be his wife, she has no choice, but I would rather be dead than be the wife of one of them brothers."

He ruffled her hair. "Don't worry. Serdin doesn't like the two brothers, and he will not let you marry either of them. He'll probably ask for ten cows as a dowry."

She picked up her basket. "I'll tell them that Serdin wants ten cows for me. That should put them off. They wouldn't be able to pay one cow."

She walked off towards the two brothers. He had a good look around to make sure he was not being attacked by raiders, then sat down and began to eat the food and drink the beer. Life was easy being an animal guard, but it was very boring. He would much rather farm the land, build huts, or hunt wild animals. He was much happier when he was doing something physical.

When he was a child, he collected eggs during the egg-laying season. He would leave at dawn to look for birds' nests, and even though he had to compete with the other children, he knew where to look and always found some eggs. He would also help to gather the crops in at harvest time. The job he liked the most was collecting wood for the fires. He would walk for long distances collecting wood.

He had now grown up and realised how complicated life was. In a few years, he would be taking a wife and building a hut and would need animals to use as barter. The bartering system was very complicated.

Serdin was the wealthiest man in the tribe and owned a huge amount of planting and grazing land. The land near their village had been cleared of trees many years ago. Half of Serdin's land was used for planting crops such as wheat and barley, and the other half was used for grazing animals. Serdin had flocks of ducks, geese and dozens of chickens. The ducks and geese had their wings clipped and were fenced in; otherwise, they would wander off into the forest and get lost. The chickens could climb over fences, but they always stayed close to their hut.

Serdin also had twenty pigs (eighteen sows and a boar), dozens of piglets, twelve cows and a bull, six calves and two bullocks for pulling the cart. Four of the cows were pregnant. He also had nineteen ewes and a ram. Most of the ewes were pregnant and would soon be giving birth. All of Serdin's animals were branded, and even though they mixed with the other animals in the village, they could always be identified. Most of the families in the village only had two or three pigs, two or three cows, two or three sheep and a few chickens.

Serdin was very good at bartering. The villagers had to pay Serdin in some way or other to have their animals guarded and put out to graze. The animals had to be penned each night; otherwise, they could be eaten by wolves or stolen. During the winter, when the snow was on the ground, the animals were kept in the pens and fed on straw. The pens did not have walls and were covered with a thatched roof, but it was warmer than being outside.

The sun was now low on the horizon. "Come on, Dip. Let's get the animals in."

Dip knew exactly what to do if one of the animals, even the bull, refused to go into the pens. Dip would bite their hooves, and Ord would prod the animal in the rear end. There was nearly always hay to eat in the pens, and sometimes, the animals would queue up to go in at night.

After putting the animals into the pens and closing the gate, Ord sat on a bench outside his father's hut and watched the sun set. Ess began talking to him, but he ignored her. No one knew where the sun went at night or where the moon went during the day. It was a mystery. What confused him was that sometimes, the moon was in the sky during the day. The sun always sets in the east and rises again in the west. Their greatest fears were that one day, the summer would not return, snow would cover the land, and they would starve to death, or the sun would not rise up, and the world would be left in darkness. The reason this did not happen was thanks to the holy man and his sacrifices to the gods made at the holy temples. It was very important to keep the gods happy.

He had been told that sometimes, when the gods were angry, the moon covered the sun, making it as dark as night. The holy man and the people then made sacrifices to the gods at the holy temples.

There were many temples all over the land, or so he had been told. Each temple had a holy man, and the people who lived within walking distance of the temple held their festivals there twice a year, once in midwinter and once in midsummer. The holiest of all the temples was called Village of the Gods (Avebury), which was two days' walk away from his village. It was the most important of the temples in the land. The one being built by Serdin, less than a day's walk away from his village, called Home of the Gods (Stonehenge), was intended to be the greatest of all the temples. It was now just a ditch and a bank around a circle of sacred healing stones. (bluestones). He had seen a model made in clay by the wise men of how Home of the Gods would look when it was finished. It would be an amazing place.

Serdin, Morteen and the wise men had already selected the ten god stones, the five lintels, the thirty protector stones and their thirty lintels that would form a circle around the god stones. They were now being shaped. It would take a few years before they were finished.

As the sun sank below the horizon, Erd, the brewer, walked towards Ord carrying a large jug of beer. He was about fifty and was one of the senior men in the village. He was also one of the biggest and tallest men in the village. "Where's Serdin?" he asked Ord.

"I don't know. Is that jug of beer for him?"

"Yes. I'll leave it by his hut." Erd placed the jug of beer by the entrance to Serdin's hut.

"I think Serdin went hunting," Ord said.

Ess pointed. "There's Serdin. He's walking towards the fire."

Erd turned to look. "Oh, yes." He picked up the jug of beer and walked off towards the fire.

Ess went into her hut, and Ord walked over to the fire. Serdin, Morteen, Old Man, and some of the senior men in the village were now sitting by the fire, eating and talking. Ord and Dip sat down behind them.

"How many temples are there in our land, Old Man?" Serdin asked. He was mean-looking and the biggest man in the village. He had a scar on his cheek. He also had a terrible temper and, if provoked, would fly into a rage.

"I don't know, Serdin," Old Man said. He was small, thin, bald, had a white beard and was the leader of the wise men in the village. "There are hundreds of holy places. Some are mounds or tombs; some are surrounded by a ditch and a bank, and some are temples with god stones or god posts."

"Which is the greatest temple of them all?" Serdin asked.

"Village of the Gods," Morteen said. He was mean-looking and almost as big as Serdin. He also had a terrible temper. He was the holy man. "It has ninety-eight god stones inside the ditch and bank. There is one large circle of god stones with two smaller circles of god stones inside it. Some of the stones are eight times as big as the healing stones."

"There's also a great temple in the far north," Old Man said. "It has a huge circle of god stones. Some of the god stones are ten times as big as the healing stones."

"I want my temple to be the greatest temple in the land," Serdin said. He took a drink from his jug of beer. "The large god stones we've selected are ten times as big as the healing stones. When will the large god stones be ready to move? They'll need to be erected first before the guardian stones are erected."

"We have men shaping them every day," Morteen said. "Most of them are ready to be moved. They should all be ready to be moved in a year. We'll have to have our holy festivals this year at Place of the Gods (Wood Henge).

"Why?" Serdin asked.

"We're in the process of pulling the healing stones down to make way for the large god stones," Morteen said.

"Don't pull all the healing stones down," Serdin said. "I get a large income from people visiting the healing stones."

Ord took a long drink of beer. He learnt a great deal from listening to the men talking. Serdin's oldest son, Leenon, guarded the healing stones and collected the goods that were given in payment by people visiting them. The visitors paid in pots, baskets, food and animals.

"Is Palace of the Gods a holy temple?" Serdin asked.

"Yes," Old Man said. "There are one hundred and eighty god posts at Place of the Gods. It's a very holy temple."

"Posts are not as good as stones," Serdin said. "The gods want stone temples that last forever and not wooden ones that rot. How long does it take to get to the great temple in the far north?"

"A whole year on foot," Old Man said. "There are many large rivers and lakes to cross. By boat, it would take about twenty days."

"I need horses," Serdin said. He took a long drink of beer. "The traveller said that he would trade horses for gold, copper, silver and tin, but not for flint. We need to mine more gold, copper, silver and tin."

"The miners are always looking for new sites to mine," Old Man said.

"It's getting near to the midsummer festival," Morteen said. "Some of the huts at Place of the Gods need repairing, and we need to build another hut."

"I'll arrange for it to be done," Serdin said.

It was now dark. Ord left the men talking and walked to his hut, followed by Dip. The day had already caught up with him, and he was almost asleep standing up.

Chapter Two

Ord was pleased when the day arrived for him to go to Place of the Gods (Wood Henge) for the midsummer festival of offerings to the gods. He set off with Dain and Erd, the brewer, and five men from his village. Erd rode on the cart that contained the provisions and the beer, and Ord led the ox that pulled the cart. The other men followed behind, and Dip ran on ahead. The sheep that was to be sacrificed and cooked at the festival was tied to the back of the cart. The roads were very bad, and Ord had to make sure that the wheels of the cart did not go into any deep holes. It was early morning, and the sun had just risen.

"I don't think it'll rain today," Ord said.

Erd looked up at the sky and nodded.

"Why are we going so early?" Ord asked. "The festival doesn't begin for another four days."

"We've been told by Serdin to help build more huts for the visitors at the festival," Erd said.

A festival could last for several days, and the worshipers slept in large huts near the temple. Serdin, Morteen, Old Man, and the senior men slept in one of the large huts and sat outside the hut in the evenings to discuss their problems. Ord always enjoyed listening to their discussions.

"Who is the beer for?" Ord asked.

"It's for us, Serdin, Morteen, Old Man and the senior men from our village," Erd said. "No one else is to have any."

"What about the wise men and the senior men from the other villages?" Ord asked. "Will they be having any?"

"No. They'll be bringing their own beer. Don't give any to the other wise men. Many men who are old claim to be wise men. We don't want to run out of beer."

"I'll make sure we don't run out of beer," Ord said.

It was slow going, and it was late in the afternoon when they reached Place of the Gods. The temple always impressed and intimidated him. Inside the ditch and the mound that encircled the temple, there were six circles of tree trunks sunk into the ground, each one representing a god or an important man. Some of the one hundred and sixty-eight tree trunks were as tall as five men. Inside the circle of tree trunks, there were two large stones and the slaughter stone where the priest sacrificed the animals.

Five of the tree trunks were taller than the others and represented the five main gods: the sun god, the god of fertility, the moon god, the god of good health and sustenance, and the god of the ancestors. The fertility god and the sun god were the two most important gods.

The cart stopped outside one of the huts that would be used by the worshipers.

Erd climbed off the cart. "Release the ox to graze and put the provisions inside this hut," he told Ord and Dain. "This is the hut we'll be sleeping in."

Dain looked about. "This holy place frightens me. I feel I'm being watched by the gods."

Ord knew exactly how he felt. He also felt intimidated by the tree trunks. "It frightens me as well. Let's get the provisions into the hut."

*

For the next three days, Ord, Dain and ten other men repaired the damaged huts and built two more large huts for the worshipers. The worshipers began to arrive on the day before Midsummer Day. In the late afternoon, Serdin, Morteen and Old Man arrived and sat around the fire with the other senior men and wise men from the other villages.

"Stay here and guard the beer and the provisions on the cart," Ord told Dain.

Dain, who had been lying on the cart, sat up. "Why? Where are you going?"

"I'm going over to the fire to give Serdin some beer." Serdin already had some beer. Ord was using it as an excuse to get near the fire so that he could hear what the men were talking about.

Ord left Dip with Dain, walked over to the fire and sat behind Serdin.

"We need to sacrifice to the gods and ask them to provide rain," one of the senior men said. "We need more rain during the summer. We lost half of our crops last year."

"The gods are angry," Morteen said. "The winter was very cold, and the snow was deep and lasted longer than normal. Many of our animals died."

"We also need to start building Home of the Gods," Serdin said. "It will please the gods."

Morteen nodded. "The gods demand god stones that last forever." He pointed to the wooden posts. "They don't want wood god posts that rot. Wood posts are fine for honouring important men, but not for honouring the gods."

"I think it's time for a human sacrifice to please the gods," one of the senior men said. "Things would be better if we sacrificed humans."

"When they sacrificed humans, who were sacrificed?" Serdin asked.

"We used to sacrifice our enemies to the gods a long time ago when we were fighting for land," Old Man said.

Ord was shocked. He had not realised that they used to sacrifice people to the gods.

Ord became bored when they started talking about gold jewellery, and he walked back to his hut. It was now dark. Dain was sitting on the cart with Dip. "I thought you'd be asleep in the hut by now, Dain."

"It's dark in the hut," Dain said. "I was waiting for you. I don't like the dark, especially when we're next to Place of the Gods."

Ord sat on the cart and stroked Dip. "Is Erd in the hut?"

"Yes." Dain looked up at the moon. "I wish I knew more about the gods and about the world. What does the moon god do?"

Ord looked up at the moon. "The moon is the god of the night and protects us from harm during the night."

"What does the god of our ancestors do?" Ord asked.

"He looks after the dead and protects us from evil spirits of the dead," Ord said. "Some of the spirits of the dead are evil, and they would harm us if we were not protected by the ancestor god."

"How many gods are there?" Dain asked.

"There are five gods. I thought everyone knew about the gods?"

"I don't," Dain said. "Who are the five gods?"

Ord took a long drink of beer. "The two main gods are the god of fertility and the sun god. They are the most important. The sun provides us with light and warmth, and the god of fertility makes sure that people and animals get pregnant. The other gods are the moon god, the god of good health and sustenance and the god of the ancestors."

"What does thunder and lightning do?" Dain asked.

"Thunder and lightning are the weapons of the gods. If the gods are angry with you, they will strike you dead with lightning. The wind is the voice of the gods."

"It's a good job we have the gods to protect us," Dain said. "If there are only five gods, why are there over a hundred posts in the temple?"

"I don't know," Ord said. "At first, I think just five god posts or god stones are put up in a holy place. Then more posts and stones are put up by important people to please the gods."

"When Serdin builds Home of the Gods, will there just be five god stones put up?" Dain asked.

"No. Home of the Gods is going to be different to any other holy place. Each of the five gods will have their own temple. They will be given a hut made of stone that has a roof and walls made of stone. The five huts will be surrounded by the healing stones. The five temples for the gods and the healing stones will be protected by a circle of guard stones, and each guard will have his own hut made of stone. It will be a fantastic temple."

Dain looked about nervously. "I can feel the gods watching us. I think I can also feel the evil spirits watching us."

Ord looked about. He also felt intimidated by the world around him, which was full of gods and the spirits of the dead. He climbed off the cart. "I'm going into the hut to sleep. Are you coming?"

Dain jumped off the cart. "Yes. I'm not staying out here on my own."

*

The banging of a drum woke Ord up. He sat up. It was still dark.

"What's that noise?" Dain asked.

"It's the drum," Ord said. "We need to get up. The festival's about to begin."

They left the hut. The light of dawn was beginning to filter into their world. The drum was a hollowed-out tree trunk and was held by two men. A third man was hitting the drum with a long piece of wood. It made a booming sound. The worshippers were emerging from the huts and gathering at the entrance to the henge.

The three men with the drum were the first to enter the huge circle of posts. They were followed by Morteen and his assistant, who was leading the sheep that was to be sacrificed and by Serdin and the senior men from the villages.

Ord was mesmerised. The only sound was the beating of the drum, which sounded like the beating of a heart. He followed the worshipers and slowly walked into the circle of posts. There were about five hundred men, women and children present.

As the sun began to rise above the horizon, Morteen raised his hands to the heavens and began to speak. The men stopped beating the drum, and Morteen's words echoed above their heads. "We offer this sacrifice to the gods. We ask that you protect us from danger and provide us with food."

The assistant placed the sheep onto the slaughter stone, and Morteen slit the sheep's throat.

"Let the festival begin," Morteen shouted.

The worshippers began shouting out their messages to the gods. Some began offering their personal offerings of flowers and food to the gods and burying the ashes of the dead. Many of the women began dancing and singing, and several fires were lit. Morteen and Serdin walked over to one of the fires.

"Come on, Dain," Ord said. "Let's go and get the beer."

They walked back to their cart. Ord left Dain to protect the beer on the cart and gave a jug of beer to Morteen and a jug to Serdin. A pig had been slaughtered and skinned. A post had been pushed through the animal, and it had been placed across the fire to cook.

Ord took out his personal jug of beer that he kept hidden under his cloak and took a long drink. Festivals to the gods made him feel vulnerable and apprehensive. It was all beyond his understanding. The more he knew about his world and the gods, the less he understood and the more confused he became.

A young woman walked up to Ord and smiled. "What's your name?" she asked.

"Ord."

"Do you have a wife, Ord?" she asked.

He shook his head.

"Would you like me to be your wife? My husband died while travelling to the festival. I like you. I don't want to be chosen by an ugly or an old man." She opened her robes to reveal her body. She had large breasts and a slim waist. "Do you like me?"

She was a very sexy woman. "Yes, but I'm not ready to take a wife. I don't have a hut, and I'm only seventeen."

She looked shocked and covered up her body. "Only seventeen. I thought you were much older."

"I'm big for my age," he said.

"You can still choose me as your wife even though you're seventeen, and I can help you build your hut."

"How old are you?" he asked.

"I'm twenty-four, but I look much younger."

"Do you have any children?" he asked.

"Yes. Three."

Ord did not want a ready-made family. "You're very beautiful, but I think you're a bit too old for me."

She sighed. "I wish women were allowed to pick their husbands. My husband, who died, was a horrible man. I'll soon be chosen by a man. I just hope he's nice and kind. Are you sure you don't want me? I'd make you a good wife."

"Yes, and I'm sorry. I hope you find a nice man."

"So do I," she said, and she walked away.

His desire for a woman was very strong, and the sight of the woman's breasts had stirred his emotions. When he returned to his village, he would begin to build a hut and then look for a wife. He would ask Serdin for some young animals. He would need some piglets, a calf, a lamb and some chickens.

The festival lasted for three days. Ord then led the cart back to his village. It was raining and he got soaked to the skin.

Chapter Three

Ord could only work building his hut before he took the animals out to graze in the morning and after he had locked them up in the pen at night, which meant working in the dark, but with Dain's help, he eventually got it done. It was a large, solidly built hut that should last for many years. He now had to do what he was dreading, and that was to ask Serdin for some young animals.

At the end of the day, Ord walked over to Serdin, who was sitting by the fire, eating. "I've finished building my hut, Serdin," Ord said.

Serdin turned to look at him. "Why are you telling me? I don't want to know about your hut."

"I intend to take a wife, and I'll need some young animals," Ord said.

"You can have some young animals, but only when you have a wife," Serdin said.

"Thank you, Serdin," Ord said, and he walked away. He did not like Serdin, and he hated talking to him.

Dain walked up to Ord. "Were you talking to Serdin?" Dain asked.

"Yes."

"What were you talking about?" Dain asked.

Ord sat down outside his hut and had a long drink of beer. "I asked him for some young animals."

Dain sat down next to him. "Why?"

"Because I want to take a wife."

"Can I sleep with you in your hut when you have a wife?" Dain asked.

"Yes. I've already told you that you can."

"Who's going to be your wife?" Dain asked.

"I don't know yet. I'll have to travel to the villages and see who's available."

Dain tucked his knees under his chin. "You won't get a good-looking wife."

"Why not?"

"Because there aren't any. There's a shortage of young women, and all the good-looking ones have gone. I know two men who are looking for a wife. I heard them say that the only ones available were a one-eyed ugly woman and a woman who looks like a man."

Ord ran his fingers through his beard. He had no intention of having an ugly wife. "I hadn't realised that there was a shortage of young women."

"If you want a wife, you will have to choose a very young girl and wait for her to grow up," Dain said. "If you choose a six-year-old to be your wife, you will have to wait for about four years for her to grow up."

"There must be some decent-looking women somewhere," Ord said. "I intend to go looking tomorrow."

"Who's going to look after the animals while you're looking for a wife?" Dain asked.

"You and the two brothers," Ord said. "I will take the animals out to pasture in the morning and bring them back to the pens in the evening, but you will have to watch them during the day. And make sure you take your bow with you."

"I will. I'm a good shot now."

*

Ord spent four days travelling with Dip to all the villages in the tribe, but he could not find a suitable woman. The only women available were very old, crippled or ugly. Even very young women had been chosen. It was late afternoon, and he was standing in a village looking at the ugliest girl he had ever seen in his life.

"You can have her for two lambs or four piglets," her father said. "She's twelve years of age and a good worker and will bear you many children."

Ord shook his head. He did not want to upset the girl by saying that she was ugly, but he would rather stay unmarried than be married to her. "She's not quite what I was looking for. Do you have any more daughters who have not been chosen?"

"Yes. I have one other daughter." He turned to look at his wife. "Where's Mud Face?"

"She's feeding the pigs," his wife said.

"Go and get her and bring her here," the man said. "And hurry up!"

The woman hurried off.

Ord frowned. "Mud Face? What sort of name is that?"

"I've forgotten what her real name is," the man said. "We call her Mud Face because she always covers her face in mud."

"What does she look like?" Ord asked. "Is she pretty?"

"No. She's worse-looking than this one. She puts mud on her face to hide the way she looks."

"Don't bother getting her," Ord said. "I'll look somewhere else."

As Ord was walking away from the village, a young girl ran after him.

"Wait," she said.

He stopped and turned around. The young girl's face was covered in mud. It was Mud Face. "What do you want?"

She stopped in front of him and began to stroke Dip. "What's his name?"

"Dip."

She looked up at him. "What's your name?"

"Ord."

"Are you looking for a wife?"

"Yes."

"I haven't been chosen," she said.

"I can understand why," he said.

"You can choose me to be your wife. If you choose me, my father will have to sell me to you."

"I don't want an ugly wife."

"I'm not ugly. I'm pretty. My grandmother, before she died, said that I was very pretty."

"You might think you're pretty, but according to your father, you're even more ugly than your sister."

"I'm not ugly," she insisted. "I'm pretty. I'd like you to choose me as your wife."

"No thanks." He turned and began to walk away. He would have to visit the neighbouring tribes to see if they had any nice-looking women who had not been chosen.

"Wait," she said. "Wait. Don't go. Just wait there."

He stopped and turned around. "Why?"

"I want to wash my face," she said as she ran off.

He did not want to upset her, but he would have to be honest and tell her that she was ugly. He watched her wash her face in the stream and then run towards him. "You're wasting your time," he said. "I have no intention of taking an ugly wife."

She threw her hair off her face and smiled up at him. "Well? What do you think? Am I pretty or ugly?"

He was amazed. She was the prettiest girl he had ever seen. "I don't understand. Your father said that you were ugly."

"It's because I pretend to be ugly," she said. "Am I pretty?"

"Yes. Your grandmother was right. You're very pretty. How do you pretend to be ugly?"

"I pull a face when I'm talking to my father, and when I talk to men who are looking for a wife. Are you going to choose me as your wife?"

He felt confused. "I don't understand. Anyone can see that you're very pretty."

"Not when I cover my face in mud and pull a face when I talk to men. Can I be your wife?"

"Why do you cover your face with mud and pull faces when you talk to men?"

"It's because I don't want to be chosen by an old man or by an ugly man. I like you, and I want you to choose me."

He now understood. "You must be very clever."

"It was my grandmother's idea. My grandmother also pretended to be ugly when she was young so that she would not get an ugly man."

"Does your mother realise what you were doing?" he asked.

"No. She's a bit of a dope. Are you going to choose me?"

He had already decided to choose her as his wife. "How old are you?"

"I'm nearly thirteen. How old are you?"

"I'm seventeen."

She smiled. "I'm just the right age for you."

She had a very beautiful smile. "What faces did you pull to make yourself look ugly?"

She looked up at him and pulled the strangest face he had ever seen. "I pull this face and talk like this when I want people to think I'm ugly."

He began to laugh. He had never seen anything so funny in his life.

She continued speaking while pulling the strange face and twisting her lips to one side. "Are you going to choose me to be your wife? I'm very pretty, don't you think?"

He was laughing so much, tears were running down his cheeks.

She smiled. "I think you like me. Am I going to be your wife?"

"Yes."

She threw her arms and legs around him and hugged him. "I'll make you a good wife. Will I be going with you today?"

"Yes. Stop hugging me, and we'll go and see your father." He scratched his chin. "If your father realises that you're pretty, he'll want a cow or even two cows for you. I don't have two cows, and I don't think I'll be able to get two cows. Pull your hair over your face, and if you have to speak, make sure you wear your funny face."

She pulled her hair over her face. "Don't worry, I will."

They walked up to her father.

"I've decided to choose Mud Face as my wife," he told her father. "What do you want for her?"

Her father looked shocked. "You want to have Mud Face as your wife?"

"Yes. I'm going to take her with me today."

"Okay," her father said. "I must warn you that she's not very bright. She can't even feed the pigs properly. I'm always moaning at her. You'd be better off with the other one."

"I want Mud Face," Ord said.

Her father spread his hands. "It's up to you. I'll accept a lamb or two piglets for her. She won't be taking anything with her except the clothes she stands up in."

"I'm not giving you that much for a retarded, ugly girl," Ord said. "I'll give you one piglet or a hen."

Her father put his hands on his hips and huffed and puffed for a while. "You're a good-looking man. Why are you prepared to take an ugly wife?"

"It's because there's a shortage of women," Ord said. "A piglet or a hen is a good offer."

"Okay," her father said. "I'll accept a hen. When will I get it?"

"I'll bring it tomorrow morning."

Ord and Mud Face walked off together. He was pleased that he had managed to get a pretty wife.

"Do you have your own hut?" she asked.

"Yes. I'll only have a few animals at first."

"What job do you do?" she asked.

"I protect the animals in the village."

"Does Dip help you?" she asked.

"Yes." He looked down at her. "You talk a lot."

She smiled. "I know."

They arrived back at the village as the sun was setting.

Dain walked up to them. "We've already penned the animals. Is this your new wife?"

"Yes," Ord said. "This is Dain, my brother. He will be sleeping with us in my hut."

"Hello, Dain," Mud Face said. "You look just like your brother."

Ord's sister, Helm, walked up to them carrying a basket. "Is this your new wife, Ord?"

"Yes," Ord said. "Did you save me some food?"

"Yes," Helm said, and she handed the basket to Ord. "What's your name?" she asked Mud Face.

"Mud Face. What's your name?"

Helm began to giggle. "My name's Helm. I'm Ord's sister. You have a very funny name."

"I know," Mud Face said.

Ord took the meat out of the basket and handed some to Mud Face. It was rabbit and bread. He sat down and began to eat the rabbit.

"We could be friends," Mud Face said to Helm.

"I'd like to be your friend, Mud Face," Helm said. "How old are you?"

"I'm nearly thirteen. How old are you?"

"I'm eight. I've also been chosen as a wife."

"It's not one of the two brothers, is it?" Ord asked.

Helm smiled. "No. It's Seend, the son of Erd. I won't be living with him until I'm a woman and I've had a show of blood. Have you had a show of blood yet, Mud Face?"

"Yes," Mud Face said.

"Can I sleep in your hut, Ord, until I go to live with Seend?" Helm asked.

"I suppose so," Ord said. "Go and get your sleeping skins. I don't have any to spare."

"I'll get them now," Helm said, and she ran off.

"I've already put my sleeping skins in your hut, Ord," Dain said.

A short time later, they all settled down in the dark hut to sleep. Dip, as usual, slept by the entrance. The beds were a layer of straw covered in a hide. In the winter, they covered themselves in furs.

He held her naked body. He had not realised how good the flesh of a young woman felt. He felt his penis slip into her. It was a fantastic feeling, and he held her body as she moved up and down.

"Is that nice?" she asked.

"Yes." It was very nice, and he felt himself beginning to climax.

"My breasts are just beginning to grow," she said. "They'll soon get big. Do you like sex?"

"Yes," he said as he climaxed. He held her tight. He had not expected sex to be so enjoyable.

She climbed off him and hugged him.

"Did you do it, Mud Face?" Helm asked.

"Yes," Mud Face said.

"I wish I had a wife," Dain said. "When I'm a bit older, will you help me build a hut, Ord?"

"Yes," Ord said. He was very tired, and he felt himself falling asleep.

"What's sex like, Mud Face?" Helm asked. "Did it hurt?"

"It was very nice and only hurt a little bit," Mud Face said.

Chapter Four

Ord felt reasonably happy with his life now that he had a wife, a hut and a few animals. Serdin had given him four hens and a cockerel, four piglets (three female and one male), a calf and a lamb. Now that he was married and had his own hut, he was paid for looking after the animals. As payment, he was given beer and food and would eventually get baskets, skins and pots. What had surprised him was discovering that Mud Face could make baskets and clothes. They had a basket maker in the village, but they did not have anyone who could make clothes, at least not well-made clothes. With just a flint knife and a bone needle, Mud Face could make coats with a hood, tunics and shoes from leather.

Late one afternoon, Ord returned to the village with the animals, just as a trader and his companions rode into the village on horseback. There was the trader, the translator, two young women, and five bodyguards armed with bows and arrows. The trader and the translator began talking to Serdin.

Leenon, Ord's brother, who was nearly as big as Serdin, walked up to Ord. He was a miserable man and a bully. He would be the next leader of the tribe when their father died, and he knew it.

He pushed Ord on the arm. "The trader and the translator and their women will be sleeping in your hut." He pointed. "You can sleep in that hut with our younger brothers and sisters. While the trader and his group are here, it'll be your job to make sure they have all they need. Dain can look after the animals."

Ord nodded. "Will I be giving them beer?"

Leenon pushed Ord on the arm. "Yes. I've just told you that they're to be given everything they need."

Leenon walked away, and Ord walked over to the fire so he could hear what his father was saying to the trader. The translator was showing Serdin some drawings on a hide, of rings, brooches, necklaces and bracelets.

"They're all made of gold and of the highest quality," the translator said. He pointed to a brooch. "This brooch was made by the Minoans, who are the most skilled workers in metal. If you're interested in any of them, the trader will bring them to you next year."

"What I need are horses," Serdin said. "Can you get me horses like yours?"

"The trader can bring you horses," the translator said. "He'll need payment in gold, silver, copper or tin."

"How much metal do I have to give for each horse?" Serdin asked.

The translator turned to the trader and spoke in a language Ord did not understand. The trader then spoke to one of the women, who walked off and returned with a leather bag. The trader opened the bag and took out some stones and pieces of wood.

Ord stepped a little closer so that he could see what they were doing.

"This machine is used to measure the weight of metals," the translator said. "They are measured in units starting from half a unit and going up to five hundred or even a thousand units. These stones are the unit stones."

"How does it work?" Serdin asked.

"I'll show you," the translator said. He assembled the pieces of wood. There was a stand that held the machine upright, a cross piece and two wooden plates hanging on a string on each side. He placed a small stone onto one of the plates. "This stone is one unit." He picked up some stones off the ground and placed one of them onto the other plate. "This one is too heavy. See how it lifts the stone of one unit up." He took the stone off and placed another stone on the plate. "This one is too light. It does not lift the stone of one unit up."

Ord was amazed. He had never seen a machine like this before. It was a very clever way to measure the weight of metal.

The translator tried several stones until he found one that was the same weight as the one-unit stone. "If this stone were gold, it would weigh one unit. For a horse, the trader would want ten units of gold, twenty units of silver, fifty units of copper and one hundred units of tin."

The translator then spoke to the trader in their foreign tongue. The translator then said, "We'll provide you with a weighing machine in exchange for food and beer while we're in your village. You'll then be able to weigh your metals and will know when you have enough for a horse."

Serdin nodded. "Make me a machine, and we'll provide you with food and beer while you're here." He opened a leather pouch. "I have some gold. Weigh this gold and tell me how many horses it will buy?"

The translator weighed the gold. It was a large amount of gold. "There's enough gold for three horses."

Serdin picked up the gold and put it back into the leather pouch. "I expected to get more horses for all this gold."

"The horses have to be trained and brought from our country across the sea," the translator said. "If they're not trained, they cannot be ridden. It's a fair price."

"I'll give you this gold when you bring me three horses," Serdin said. "I want two females and one male."

The translator spoke to the trader, and he nodded his head. "The trader will bring you the three horses next year. Before travelling back to our land, we'll be travelling to the tribe north of you, near where the Village of the Gods temple is."

Ord walked back to his hut.

"Who are they?" Mud Face asked.

"They're traders," Ord said. "They'll be sleeping in our hut, so we'll have to sleep with my younger brothers and sisters." He turned to Helm. "Take food and beer in your basket for the traders and make sure they have all they want. If they ask for anything other than food and beer, come and see me."

"I will," Helm said.

When it began to get dark, the villagers went into their huts. Ord had expected all of the trading party to sleep in his hut, but the bodyguards remained outside next to the twelve horses they had with them.

Ord and Mud Face went into the hut where his younger brothers and sisters slept.

"It smells in here," Mud Face said.

"I know," he said.

*

It had been a cramped and uncomfortable night in the crowded hut with his brothers and sisters. Ord was glad when dawn came, and he was able to leave the hut and stretch his limbs. He had not had sex. Mud Face said that she was sore.

Dip looked at the horses and growled.

Ord ruffled Dip's fur. "Calm down. They won't hurt us. They're just horses."

Mud Face walked out of the hut. She looked about and frowned. "Who were you talking to?"

"I was talking to Dip. Come with me. We need to make sure that Helm has meat, beer and bread ready for the traders."

She followed him. "As long as there's some for me. I'm starving."

When the trader and the translator came out of Ord's hut and began to warm themselves by the fire, Helm gave them some food and beer. Ord envied the traders who travelled all over the world. They were talking in their foreign language. Ord would love to know what they were saying.

When the travellers were preparing to leave, one of Serdin's dogs barked at the horses, and one of the horses kicked out at the dog. The translator was behind the horse, and the hoof caught him in the back, and he fell to the ground. The translator was conscious, but he did not try to get up. The trader began talking to the translator in their foreign language.

"Why doesn't he get up?" Mud Face asked.

"I don't know," Ord said. "He was kicked very hard, and his back could be broken."

"If he has a broken back, he'll never be able to walk again," Mud Face said.

"I know," Ord said.

Serdin walked over to the injured translator. "What's wrong?"

"I've been injured, and I can't move my legs," the translator said. "I'll need to rest for a few days."

The trader began speaking to the translator. Everyone stood watching. It seemed as if they were arguing about something. Eventually, the translator said to Serdin, "The trader needs me to go with him to the other tribe to translate for him. Could we borrow your cart? I would be able to travel on the cart. We would need the cart for about five days. The trader said that he'll bring you four horses instead of three for your gold if you do."

Serdin nodded. "Yes. Tell him he can borrow my cart." He turned to Ord. "Go and get the cart ready. You can lead the cart."

"Yes, Serdin," Ord said.

Ord was pleased. He had never travelled to the tribe to the north, and he would love to see the Village of the Gods.

"Can I come with you, Ord?" Mud Face asked.

"No. You'll need to look after the animals with Dain."

When Ord had the cart hitched up to the ox and loaded with the provisions they would need for five days, he carefully lifted the translator onto the cart. "Are you in pain?" Ord asked the translator.

"Yes. My back hurts. What I don't like is not being able to move my legs. If I could move my legs, I could ride a horse."

The trader, the two women and the bodyguards rode out of the village on horseback, and Ord followed them, leading the ox and the cart. Dip ran on ahead.

The trader shouted something.

"We need to go faster," the translator said to Ord. "Go as fast as you can."

"It'll be very bumpy," Ord said.

"It doesn't matter," the translator said. "We don't want to upset the trader."

After travelling for one day, Ord spent the night sleeping on the back of the cart with Dip, the translator and his woman. At dawn, they continued their journey. They were now in the land of the other tribe.

"Is it dangerous to travel all over the world?" Ord asked the translator.

"Yes. It can be very dangerous, which is why we have men to protect us. You also carry a bow. How good are you with it?"

"Very good. Have you been attacked in our land?"

"No. We've been attacked in my land across the sea and in far distant lands."

The translator was holding onto the sides of the cart. Even though Ord was being as careful as he could in trying to avoid the deep holes in the road, the translator was still being bounced up and down as they travelled.

"Are you still in pain?" Ord asked.

"Yes." The translator grimaced. "The pain's very bad. The horse's hoof has cut deep into my back. I should be resting. If it gets infected, I will die."

"You probably just need a few days' rest," Ord said.

The translator looked worried. "Even if my back heals, I don't think I'll be doing any more travelling."

"Why not?" Ord asked.

"I still can't feel my legs or move them. I've seen this happen before. A back or a neck injury can leave a man paralysed. I don't think I'll ever walk again."

"How will you travel back to your land?" Ord asked.

"I don't know. If my back heals, I might be able to ride a horse. We shall have to wait and see."

It was early evening when they reached the village where the leader of the other tribe lived, and the sun was beginning to leave their world.

A tall, strong-looking man walked up to the cart. "I'm Dromda, the leader of this tribe," the tall man said to the translator. "Will you ask the trader if he's brought me the gold ring and the bracelets that I asked him to bring?"

The trader and the translator began to speak to each other in their language. The trader then gave Dromda a leather purse. Dromda opened the purse and looked at the ring and the bracelets.

"Do you like them?" the translator asked Dromda.

"Yes," Dromda said. "Why are you lying on the cart?"

"I hurt my back. Do you have the gold?"

"Yes," Dromda said. "I have the gold."

The trader took the gold from Dromda, weighed it on his machine, and then spoke to the translator. "The trader has accepted the payment," the translator said to Dromda. "The ring and the bracelets are now yours. We'll spend the night in your village and then leave in the morning."

"You'll be safe here," Dromda said, and he walked away.

Ord did not like Dromda. He looked to be a dangerous man. "Can you trust, Dromda?" Ord asked the translator.

"We cannot trust anyone," the translator said. "Keep your bow near to you." He looked at Dip. "Is he a good guard dog?"

"Yes. Dip will warn us if someone comes near to us during the night. Where is the Village of the Gods?"

"It's only a short distance away to the north."

Ord and Dip climbed onto the cart. Ord decided to have a look at the Village of the Gods in the morning before they left, if he had time.

*

Ord was up at dawn, and while he was having breakfast, the translator had a long discussion with the trader. The trader, his guards and one of the women climbed onto their horses and rode off.

"What's happening?" Ord asked the translator. "Where are they going?"

"The trader's going back to our land. Me and my woman will be staying in your village until my back gets better. My woman will ride her horse. You can tie my horse to the back of the cart."

Ord tied the horse to the back of the cart. "Do we have to hurry, or can we take our time?"

"There's no need for us to hurry. Try to avoid the deep holes."

They started their return journey at a much slower pace than before.

Ord had noticed that Dramda pronounced some words differently from him, and he had only just been able to understand what he was saying. "How many languages are there in the world?" Ord asked the translator.

"I don't know. There could be hundreds. I can speak four languages fluently, and I can understand another four languages."

"I noticed that Dromda sometimes used different words to me," Ord said. "He's in my land, and so he should speak like me."

"Each of the tribes in your land speaks slightly differently," the translator said. "The tribe to your southwest, where they have a lot of tin mines, speak almost a different language to you."

"I would like to speak another language," Ord said. "How do I say, what is your name in your language?"

The translator spoke a few words. "That's how you say, what is your name?"

Ord turned to the woman and spoke the foreign words.

The woman smiled and said, "Sena."

Ord turned to the translator and spoke the same foreign words.

The translator smiled and said, "Bruna."

Ord had an idea. "If you teach me to speak your language, I'll provide you both with food and beer while you stay in my village."

"It's very difficult to learn another language, and it takes a long time," Bruna said. "I tried to teach the trader, but he could not do it. Only a few men can speak in another language."

"How long will you be staying in my village?" Ord asked.

"At least ten days," Bruna said.

"I'll learn your language in ten days," Ord said.

Bruna smiled. "That would be impossible, but I'll teach you some words. Why do you want to learn my language?"

"I'd like to be a trader like you and travel all over the world."

"I'm not a trader," Bruna said. "I'm just a translator."

"What is your word for horse?" Ord asked.

During the three days travelling to his village, Bruna taught Ord many foreign words. When they arrived in the village, Ord released the ox and the horse so that they could graze.

"What are you going to do, Bruna?" Ord asked.

"What do you mean?"

"Are you going to stay on the cart, or do you want to sit by the fire?"

"I'll sit by the fire during the day and sleep in your hut at night," Bruna said.

Ord carried Bruna to the fire and laid him down on the ground. "I'll get you and Sena some food and beer," Ord said.

Mud Face ran up to Ord. "What's happening? Why is that man and woman here?"

"They're staying here until his back gets better. His name's Bruna, and her name's Sena. Have you been looking after the animals?"

"Yes."

"Get me some food and beer," Ord said. "Also, get Bruna and Sena some food and beer. We'll be feeding them while they're here. Where's Dain?"

"He's looking after the grazing animals with the two brothers."

Chapter Five

For fifteen days, Ord and Mud Face spent the evenings sitting by the fire with Bruna and Sena, learning their language. Ord could now speak it fluently, and Mud Face could just about understand what was being said. The four of them had become friends.

Ord had just penned the animals in for the night and was sitting by the fire with Bruna, Sena and Mud Face.

"When are you going home, Bruna?" Ord asked in Bruna's language. They now only spoke to each other in Bruna's foreign language.

"I don't know. My back's healed, but I still can't move my legs."

"Do you think you could ride a horse?" Ord asked.

"If you could ride a horse, we could go home," Sena said. She was pregnant. "I don't want to give birth in this land."

"I'll miss you when you go," Mud Face said.

Bruna looked up at the trees. "The leaves are turning brown, and winter's coming. We really need to start back now. It'll be very difficult to travel when there is snow on the ground." He turned to look at Ord. "Could you help me get on my horse? I think I could ride."

Ord stood up. "Yes. I'm sure you can ride. I'll go and get your horse."

Ord and Dain helped Bruna onto his horse. Bruna was able to keep his balance, but when the horse moved, he fell off.

"Do you want to get back on the horse and try again?" Ord asked.

"No," Bruna said. "It would be a waste of time. I don't think I'll ever be able to ride a horse again. You need feelings in your legs to ride a horse."

Ord picked Bruna up and carried him to the fire. "Do you have any feelings in your legs?"

"No, and I can't move them."

Sena looked upset. "Then what are we going to do? How are we going to get home?"

Bruna blew out his cheeks. "I don't know. I don't want to spend the rest of my life here, but what can I do?"

"You could travel by cart to the coast and then get on a boat," Ord said.

"I could, but when I get off the boat in my land, I would need another cart to travel to my village," Bruna said. "Carts are not easy to get."

"How big are boats that travel across the sea?" Ord asked. "I've only ever seen riverboats. Could you get the cart on a sea boat?"

"Some sea boats are very big," Bruna said. "You could get a cart and an ox and eight horses on a big sea boat."

"Then let's take the cart," Sena said. "You could buy the cart off Serdin?"

Bruna sat thinking for a while. "I don't know. He might not want to sell the cart, but even if I bought it, I would need someone to lead the cart. And we'd need a guard; otherwise, we will be robbed. I'll not be able to fight off a robber."

"You could ask Ord to come with us?" Sena said. "He could lead the cart and protect us."

Bruna looked at Ord. "What do you think? Would you be willing to travel with us?"

"I don't know. You want me to travel with you all the way to your village?"

"Yes," Bruna said. "I can trust you. What do you think?"

Ord would love to travel across the sea to a foreign land. "Can you afford to buy the cart and the ox off Serdin?"

"Yes. Will Serdin sell them?"

"I think he will," Ord said. "He could always get another cart built. When would you be leaving?"

"As soon as possible. It'll take at least ten days to get to my land. It could take fifteen days. If you come with us, I'll give you my horse. You can ride the horse back here. I'll also give you some gold to pay the boatman to take you back across the sea to your land."

Ord looked at the horse. He would love to own a horse. "You'll have to have a word with Serdin first. If he does sell you the cart and the ox, I will go with you."

"And what about me?" Mud Face asked.

"What do you mean?" Ord asked.

"I want to go with you," Mud Face said. "I don't want to stay here on my own."

"If you come, who will look after the animals and the hut?" Ord asked.

"Dain and Helm can look after the animals and the hut," Mud Face said. "I don't like sleeping alone."

Ord did not want to take Mud Face with him. "I'll only be away for fifteen days at the most."

"You could be away for more than fifteen days," Mud Face said. "If the snows begin when you're in the foreign land, you will have to wait there until the spring before travelling back here."

"Why not take her with you?" Bruna said. "A man needs a woman to sleep with at night, which is why I always take Sena with me."

Ord did like sleeping with Mud Face in his arms. "I suppose I could take you."

Mud Face smiled. "It'll be an exciting adventure."

"You can ride Bruna's horse, Mud Face," Sena said.

Mud Face looked at the horse. "I don't know how to ride a horse."

"I'll teach you to ride," Sena said.

"Can you teach me to ride as well?" Ord asked.

"Yes. I can teach both of you."

*

Serdin agreed to let Ord and Mud Face go with Bruna, and he accepted a piece of gold for the cart and the ox. Ord and Mud Face then spent the day learning to ride a horse, and by the time the sun was setting, they were riding as if they had been born in the saddle.

The next day at dawn, loaded with provisions, they headed south with Bruna on the cart. Sena and Mud Face were riding the horses, Ord was leading the ox, and Dip was running on ahead. Dain and Helm were going to look after Ord's animals while they were away, so there should not be any problems.

There was a smile on Ord's face. He had never been so happy. His dream of seeing the world was coming true. "Where will we be catching the sea boat, Bruna?"

"We'll follow the river to the sea. There's a village there, and the large sea boats are moored there."

"Do you trade with the leaders of all the tribes in this land?" Ord asked.

"No. Only the wealthy tribes in the south of your land."

"How do you know where their villages are?" Ord asked.

"We have a map."

Ord did not know anything about maps. "Can I see this map?"

"Yes. I have maps of the entire world written on hides."

Ord stopped the ox, sat down on the cart, took a drink of beer and then looked at the map of his land that Bruna had given him. "Could you explain what the drawings are? I don't understand maps."

Bruna pointed. "This is land, and this is the sea. These lines are the rivers, and the circles are the tribes. The dots are the villages where the leaders of the tribes live."

Ord was amazed. "My land is surrounded by sea."

"Yes. Your land is a large island. To the west of your land, there is a smaller island. We trade with two tribes on that island."

"There are hundreds of tribes in my land," Ord said. "Which one is my tribe?"

Bruna pointed to one of the circles. "This one." He handed Ord another skin. "This is a map of the world."

Ord looked at the map. It was even more confusing than the map of his land. "I can see what is land and what is sea and where the rivers are, but what are the little circles?"

"They are the tribes." He pointed. "This is your land."

Ord was amazed. "That little island is my land?"

"Yes."

"The world must be a very big place," Ord said. "Where is your land?"

He pointed. "This is my land. I live here in this village. They say there is only sea to the west of my land. The shape of the land north of my land, which is covered in snow, is not known. The land to the south of my land is where the Minoans and the Egyptians live. They also say that the land east of my land goes on forever."

"I didn't realise that the world was so big," Ord said. "Could I make copies of these maps?"

"Yes. We'll make some copies when we stop for the night."

They continued their journey, and Ord began to wonder about his world. The more he knew about it, the more confused he became. The world was a very large place.

*

They spent the night sleeping on the cart and, after grazing the animals in the morning, continued to the coast. It was raining, and they had their hoods up. They met a few other travellers who were on foot, but they ignored them.

Bruna had given gold for the cart and the ox, and Ord suspected that he carried a large amount of gold with him. "Do you live in the same village as the trader?" Ord asked Bruna.

"Yes."

"What is the trader like?"

"He's the head man in our village and a very powerful man. He has a violent temper."

"How do you get paid for being a translator?"

"I get a small percentage of what the trader makes. He's a fair man."

"Who makes the gold ornaments and jewellery that you trade?"

"There are only a few really talented metalworkers in the world. There are none in your land. We have one in our village, and there are two that we know of in the land of the Minoans. There are also some in the land of Egypt where they build the biggest tombs in the world."

"How big are these tombs?"

Bruna pointed. "They're ten times bigger than that tree, and they're made of large blocks of rock."

Ord turned to look at the tree. Sometimes men exaggerated, and he believed that Bruna was exaggerating. Nothing could be ten times as big as that tall tree.

It was late in the day, and the sun was beginning to set, when they reached the boat builder's village by the sea. It was a large village with about forty huts.

A man walked towards them. He was a large man and looked to be very strong. "Will you be wanting to travel across the sea?" he asked.

"Yes," Bruna said. "Where is Steen, the man who owns the big seagoing boat?"

"He's away at sea," the man said. "We expect him back tomorrow. Why are you lying in the cart?"

"I was kicked by a horse. When you see Steen, will you tell him that I want to travel across the sea with this cart and ox, two horses and four people?"

"Do you have gold?" the man asked.

"Yes, I have gold," Bruna said.

"You can stay in the village," the man said. He pointed. "You can sleep in that hut that we keep for travellers." He turned and walked off.

"Who was that?" Ord asked.

"He's the leader of the tribe."

Ord counted ten armed men in the village. "Are we safe here?"

"Yes. We will not be harmed in this village. They make a good living from travellers, and it would be foolish to harm them."

Mud Face and Sena climbed off their horses.

"Where is the sea?" Mud Face asked.

Bruna pointed. "Over that ridge."

Ord and Mud Face walked to the top of the ridge.

Ord was amazed by the sight of the sea. He had never seen anything like it before. "Look at all that water," he said. "I didn't realise that the sea would look like that."

"It's very big," Mud Face said. "Is there land on the other side of the sea?"

"Yes. It's where Bruna and Sena live."

Mud Face looked worried. "Are we going to travel over that sea in a boat?"

"Yes. The water is very lumpy, and it's moving up and down. It's nothing like a river. I wonder how big the boats are that travel over the sea."

They walked back to the cart.

"Do you want to sit by the fire, Bruna?" Ord asked.

"No. The ground will be wet. I'll spend the night here on the cart."

It was beginning to get dark. Sena settled down with Bruna on the cart, and Ord, Mud Face, and Dip went into the hut. It smelt like a cesspit.

"I think they use this as a toilet," Ord said. "I'm not sleeping in here."

They walked back out of the hut.

"We're going to sleep on the cart with you, Bruna," Ord said.

"Why?" Bruna asked. "What's wrong with the hut?"

"It smells like a cesspit."

Ord and Mud Face climbed onto the cart and lay down on their sleeping skins.

Chapter Six

In the morning, Ord went to watch the men building a huge boat near where the river flowed into the sea. They had built the floor of the boat out of long planks of wood and were building the sides. It was about twelve paces long and about five paces wide.

"Is this a seagoing boat?" Ord asked the man who was working on the boat.

"Yes. It'll be one of the biggest boats to ever sail on the sea."

"I've only ever seen a riverboat before," Ord said. "I know how they split the planks from a tree and shape them with flint axes, but how do you join the planks together?"

"We use rope," the man said.

"Do sea boats leak?" Ord asked.

"Yes. All boats leak. "You have to bail out the water continually. When we build them, we keep the wood dry, which is why we have a roof over this boat. When we put the boat on the river, the wood gets wet and swells up. It then fills the gaps and stops most of the leaks."

"How will you get the boat to the sea when you've built it?" Ord asked. "It looks too heavy to drag."

"It would be impossible to drag," the man said. He pointed. "We dig away that bank and let the river water in and float the boat onto the river. We can then sail it into the harbour."

"Do these boats have ores like the riverboats?" Ord asked.

"Yes. They have ores and steer the boat with a big ore. They also have sails made of animal skins. When the wind blows onto the skins, it moves the boat along."

"I'm travelling across the sea in one of these boats," Ord said. "Are they safe?"

"Yes, for most of the time. Sometimes, they sink in a storm."

Ord walked back to the cart. He was not looking forward to travelling across the sea. He sat down on the cart next to Bruna. "Are you a wealthy man, Bruna?"

"Yes."

"When I've taken you to your village, I'll need to get back to my village," Ord said. "How much does it cost to travel across the sea?"

"It costs one unit of gold, a sheep, or a pig. I'll give you one unit of gold to pay the boatman."

"I'll also need some provisions for the journey," Ord said.

"I'll give you provisions as well."

"Are you getting any feelings in your legs?"

"No. I don't think I will ever walk again."

"Who will the trader get to translate for him?" Ord asked.

"There's another man in our village who can understand languages."

*

They had to wait five days for the sea boat to return. The men who sailed the boat wanted to rest before sailing again, and it was a further three days before they began loading the boat. The cart was put onto the boat first. They then blindfolded the ox and the horses and led them onto the boat. It was obvious that the horses did not like being on a boat.

"I don't want to travel on a boat across the sea," Mud Face said to Ord.

"I don't either, but it's something we have to do. I'm eager to see what other countries look like."

"We could be in danger in this foreign land," Mud Face said. "I could get raped or murdered."

He squeezed her arm. He could understand her fear. He was also apprehensive. "Don't worry. I will protect you. No one will ever rape you or hurt you."

She looked up at him. "Will you really protect me?"

"Yes. I will always protect you."

When the horses and the ox had had their legs tied together and had been made to lie down in the boat, Ord carried Bruna onto the boat and placed him on the cart.

"What happens if the boat sinks?" Ord asked.

Bruna smiled. "We will all drown. Your dog will live because he can swim, but unless you can swim, you will drown."

"I don't think I can swim," Ord said.

"And I know I can't swim," Mud Face said.

"Don't worry, Mud Face," Sena said. "The boat will not sink."

Ord sat down next to Mud Face, Sena and Dip. The boat was moving about, and Ord held onto the cart. The bottom of their boat was filled with water that came up to his ankles.

"I don't like being on a boat," Mud Face said. "I don't like the way the boat goes up and down."

"You'll get used to it after a while," Sena said. "I like sailing on the sea."

The three men who would be sailing the boat climbed on board. Two of the men picked up an oar and began rowing, and the boat moved out into the sea. The other man steered the boat with a large oar.

The man steering the boat pointed to several large beakers. "Use those beakers to throw the water in the bottom of the boat overboard. You'll have to keep bailing out the water while you're in the boat; otherwise, we will sink."

Ord, Sena and Mud Face began to bail out the water.

"I didn't realise that seawater moved up and down so much," Ord said to Bruna.

"There are always waves on the sea," Bruna said. "Sometimes the waves are very big and come into the boat. When there's a storm, the waves can be three or four times taller than a man, which is why we never sail on the sea when the weather's bad."

Ord began to feel sick. "How long will we be in the boat?"

"We'll travel east and stay near the land for one day, and then spend the night on the land. If the weather's good, we'll then travel across the sea to my land, which will take one day."

The men erected two poles with hides tied to them. When the wind blew into the hides, it pushed the boat along, and the men did not need to row. Ord did not like being on a sea boat and would much rather feel his feet on solid ground.

Late in the afternoon, the boat sailed into a cove. The men tied the boat to a wooden platform and led the animals off the boat. Ord was relieved to feel the solid ground beneath his feet. They lit a fire and had a meal of bread and cheese, and then crawled into a hut to sleep.

Mud Face snuggled up to him. "I like to be with you, but I wish I'd stayed in your village. I hate sailing on the sea. It frightens me and makes me feel sick."

"It makes me feel sick as well," he said. He pulled her into his arms. "I'm glad I brought you with me. I'd feel lost without my little Mud Face."

"I didn't mean what I said," she said. "I'd rather be with you, even if it does mean sailing on the sea."

*

At dawn, they began to load the boat. Ord looked out to sea. There was supposed to be a land across the sea, although he could not see it. When they had loaded the boat and put the animals on board, they climbed onto the boat. The boat sailed out to sea and began to move up and down. Ord began to bail out the water. He felt sick and now wished he had not agreed to take Bruna back to his land. He had a bad feeling about this adventure.

When they were in the middle of the sea, some of the waves began to wash into the boat, and everyone except Bruna began to bail out the water.

"I think we're going to die," Mud Face said.

"Just keep bailing out the water," Ord said.

"We can now see my land," Bruna said, and he pointed.

Ord sat up and looked into the distance. "It still looks far away."

"We'll soon be there," Bruna said. "The wind's blowing in the right direction and filling the sails."

It was late in the afternoon when they sailed into a harbour.

"This is where you will catch the boat when you return to your land," Bruna said.

Ord helped to get the animals and the cart off the boat. When he did return to his land, he would never leave it again. Sailing on the sea was not for him.

When they were eating their meal around the fire, Bruna gave the boatman a unit of gold for taking them across the sea and then gave Ord a unit of gold. "This is to pay for your return journey across the sea. Keep it safe. I'll not be giving you any more."

Ord leant nearer to Bruna and whispered, "Are you carrying a large amount of gold with you?"

Bruna nodded. "I'm relying on you to protect us if we meet up with robbers."

"I'll protect you," Ord said. "How long will it take us to reach your village from this village?"

"It takes five days on horseback. In this cart, it'll probably take us ten or twelve days."

Mud Face looked about at the village. "The land, the huts and the people look the same as they do in our land."

"Yes, until the people speak," Ord said. "Do they speak your language all across your land?"

"Yes, although it's slightly different in the far north and in the south."

It began to rain, and Ord carried Bruna into a hut with a roof and no walls. "Why don't they put walls on their huts?"

"They only use these huts for travellers," Bruna said.

Ord lay down to sleep, and Mud Face crawled into his arms. "I can't believe what's happened to me," she said. "There I was feeding the chickens and the pigs and worrying about being married to an ugly or an old man, and now I'm married to the most handsome man who has ever lived, and I've just travelled across the sea to another land."

"I know what you mean," he said. "A short time ago, I was looking after animals and had a very boring life. My life is anything but boring now, and I'll soon be the owner of a horse."

"Do you want me to rub your rod?" she asked.

"No. I'm too tired."

*

They started their journey at dawn. Mud Face and Sena were riding the horses; Bruna was sitting on the cart; Ord was leading the ox, and Dip was running ahead. The roads were just as bad as in his land, and the countryside looked exactly like his countryside.

"I know we were safe in the village, but are we safe travelling in your land?" Ord asked.

"If we were travelling with the trader and his armed guards, I don't think we'd be robbed, but we're just a crippled man on a cart with two women and with just one guard. I'm very worried. All the people in the village we just left will know how vulnerable we are, and some of them might try to rob us. If they did, they would get two horses, the ox, the cart and my gold."

"They wouldn't know you had gold," Ord said.

"They know that I'm a translator, and they'll assume I have some gold. Just keep ready with your bow. How many arrows do you have?"

"Thirty. I carry two quivers with fifteen arrows in each one."

"You said that you were good with a bow," Bruna said. "Just how good are you?"

"Very good. I could hit a man at twenty paces every time. And I could hit a man at thirty paces with four out of every five arrows."

"Have you ever shot a man?" Bruna asked.

"No."

"You need more than just accuracy," Bruna said. "You also need to be brave. If you're a nervous man and you're attacked, they will kill you. Not all men are brave."

"I am," Ord said. "I'm frightened of no man."

"I'm pleased to hear that," Bruna said.

Mud Face looked worried. "What should me and Sena do if we are attacked?"

"If we're attacked, jump off your horse and hide," Ord said. "I don't want you getting shot."

As they travelled along, they passed several travellers who were on foot. When it became too dark to travel, they slept on the cart. With Dip with them, there was no way they would be taken by surprise by robbers during the night; nevertheless, Ord slept with his bow in his hand.

*

At dawn, they continued their journey. Mud Face and Sena chatted about babies and how best to look after them. Ord was only half listening; he was too worried about being attacked. By the afternoon, Ord was beginning to relax. "I think we're safe now, Bruna."

"We're not safe yet," Bruna said. "From now on, we must be very careful. If we're going to be attacked, it will be today or tomorrow. They would not risk attacking us near their village."

"We've never been attacked before in our land," Sena said.

"That's because I wasn't crippled, and we had several armed guards," Bruna said.

"If we're attacked, we'll be safe with Ord to protect us," Mud Face said. "Ord's a very big man."

"A big man can be shot with an arrow as easily as a small man," Bruna said. He pointed. "Look." An old man and a woman were walking towards them along the road.

"It's only an old man and a woman, and the man is not armed," Mud Face said.

The man and the woman walked up to them.

The man smiled. "Good day, fellow travellers," he said. "Do you have far to travel?"

Ord was pleased that he could understand what he had said.

"Yes," Bruna said. "We have ten days ahead of us."

The man and the woman walked off.

Bruna looked very worried. "We will be attacked before nightfall."

Ord frowned. "How can you possibly know that?"

"That man and woman we passed were checking us out. I wish I'd learnt how to use a bow. I tried it once. I was useless. I would only be able to hit a man if he were standing in front of me."

Ord looked about. "You could be wrong."

"I don't think so," Bruna said. "There will be four, five or even six men. Make sure you kill as many as you can."

"Will they ambush us?" Ord asked.

"I don't know," Bruna said. "We'll have to wait and see."

"Sena, Mud Face," Ord said. "Get off your horses and walk with them, and if we're attacked, lie down on the ground."

Sena and Mud Face climbed off their horses.

"I'm feeling frightened," Mud Face said. "What if we're attacked by five armed men?"

"I can handle five men," Ord said.

Bruna frowned. "How can you defeat five armed men?"

"I'm very good and fast with a bow," Ord said.

"What will happen if we're attacked by ten or more men?" Mud Face asked.

"I'll probably be killed," Ord said.

"You're very confident, but I don't think you will be able to defeat five armed men," Bruna said. "Let's hope we're attacked by just two or three men. We might then stand a chance."

"Let's hope that we're not attacked by any men," Sena said. "I'm beginning to feel frightened."

"What I'm worried about is being ambushed," Ord said. "If I can't see them, I can't kill them. What do you think, Bruna? If we are attacked, will we be ambushed?"

"I don't know," Bruna said. "Just keep a good lookout just in case."

In the distance, four men appeared and began to walk towards them along the road.

"We're not going to be ambushed," Bruna said. "We're going to be attacked by four men, and they're armed."

"Mud Face, Sena, get behind the cart," Ord said.

Sena and Mud Face hid behind the cart. They looked frightened.

Ord walked in front of the cart and put an arrow to his bow. Dip stood by his side.

"They look confident because they only have one man to deal with," Bruna said.

Behind the four armed men, Ord could see the old man and the woman they had passed on the road. "You were right, Bruna. The man and the woman were sizing us up."

"Just kill as many as you can," Bruna said.

"There's no need to worry, Bruna," Ord said. "I won't have a problem killing all four of them."

The four men stopped in front of them.

"We will not kill you if you give us your horses, the cart and the ox," the tallest of the men said.

"If I were you, I would turn around and walk away," Ord said. "This is not a good day to die."

The tall man smiled. "I would take your own advice and walk away. This is not a good day to die. You are too young to die."

Ord pointed to the woman who was watching them. "Is that your woman?"

Without turning around, the tall man said, "Yes. Are you going to walk away?"

"You're a fool," Ord said. "Your woman's about to watch you die."

Ord began shooting the four men. A short time later, the four men were lying writhing on the ground. One had been shot in the eye, and the other three had been shot in the throat. Ord ran to the men, took out his flint knife and cut their throats.

Ord stood up and looked about. The old man and the woman had disappeared. "I think there were only four men." He frowned. Sena, Mud Face and Bruna were staring at him with their mouths and eyes wide open. "What's wrong?"

"I've never seen anything like it in my life," Bruna said. "It's not possible to shoot an arrow as fast as you did and as accurately. You killed the four men before they could shoot an arrow at you. How did you do it?"

Ord grinned. "I told you I was good. When I was looking after the animals, all I did all day was practice with my bow."

"You're the best bowman I've ever seen by far," Bruna said. "Search them and see if they have anything worth taking."

Ord searched the men. They were poor men and had nothing of value on them. "They have nothing worth taking."

"What about their bows and arrows?" Bruna said.

Ord examined the bows and the arrows. "The bows are of poor quality. I'll take the arrows. They only had three arrows each."

"Why did you shoot three of them in the neck and one in the eye?" Mud Face asked.

"I shot the one in the eye by mistake. I was aiming for his neck."

Bruna shook his head. "You actually aimed for their necks?"

"Yes. I can now say that I've killed four men. I've also proved that I'm a brave man."

"You're very brave," Mud Face said. "I was terrified."

"I was as well," Sena said. "I thought we were going to die. I didn't realise that one man could kill four men."

"If I were you, I would take their bows as well," Bruna said. "If you break your bow, we will be helpless."

Ord chewed his lip for a few moments. "Their bows are almost useless, but you're right. If I broke my bow, we would be helpless."

"What's wrong with their bows?" Bruna asked. "They look just like your bow."

Ord picked up one of their bows and stood it next to his bow. "They are not as thick as my bow or as long, and they're made of the wrong wood. They should have used wood from the yew tree." He placed the three bows into the cart. "I'll keep the bows just in case, but I think I'll make a new bow."

Ord walked over to a yew tree and cut off a suitable branch for his new bow. "I'll make the bow when we stop for the night."

Bruna frowned. "Are you a bowmaker as well as a bowman? It takes a skilled man to make a bow."

"I know," Ord said. "We have a very skilled bowmaker in our village, but his bows and arrows are very expensive, and I could never afford them. When I was young, I used to help him gather the wood for his bows and arrows, and I learnt about what wood to select. I used to watch him making his bows and arrows, and I can now make a bow and an arrow as good as the ones he makes. I also watched him make the bowstring, but I could never do it as good as him, so I bought several bowstrings from him. I always carry them with me."

"You're an amazing young man," Bruna said.

Ord grinned. "I know. Mud Face and Sena, get back on your horses. Let's continue our journey."

"I feel much safer now," Sena said. "Having Ord to guard us is as good as having six guards."

"More like ten guards," Bruna said. "I also feel much safer now."

When it became too dark to travel, they stopped under a huge tree and settled down on the cart to sleep. There was a smile on Ord's face. He now felt that he had proved he was a man, even though he was only seventeen.

Chapter Seven

It was a long and difficult journey to Bruna's village, and it took a total of fifteen days. They saw many travellers on their journey, but they were not attacked again. By the time they walked into Bruna's village, Ord had made two spare bows.

They were greeted by the trader, who was the leader of the village. "I didn't expect to see you again, Bruna," the trader said. "Are you still unable to walk?"

"Yes, Vistern. I don't think I'll ever walk again."

Vistern pointed to two men. "Help Bruna get off the cart and place him near the fire."

Ord looked about. The village was very big and consisted of about thirty-five huts. Ord and Mud Face sat down by the fire next to Bruna and Vistern. The smell of the meat cooking made Ord's mouth water.

"We're eating beef tonight, Bruna," Vistern said. "It was to celebrate your return. When I was told that you had returned, I was hoping that you'd recovered and were able to walk. I'm very disappointed. I'm lost without a translator. I was hoping to travel to the Minoans and to Egypt. The Egyptians will provide a translator, but I prefer to have one of my own."

"What about the young translator?" Bruna asked. "He can speak four languages."

"He died," Vistern said. "He had some strange illness and dropped down dead."

"When were you intending to travel to Egypt?" Bruna asked.

"As soon as possible, Vistern said. "I was waiting for you to arrive. It's now late in the year. I was hoping to start the journey now and reach the coast before the snow became deep. I then intended to travel by boat to the Minoans and then on to Egypt. Their summers are blisteringly hot, but their winters are warm and more like our summers. I have many orders for jewellery, rings, brooches, necklaces, and bracelets from the Minoans, and I was also hoping to trade silver for gold with the Egyptians."

"You could ask Ord to be your translator," Bruna said. "He has a gift for languages."

"He'll have to speak three languages as well as his own language, and I don't have time to wait," Vistern said.

"I can already speak your language," Ord said. He spoke in Vistern's language.

Vistern looked shocked. "When did you learn my language?"

"Bruna taught me when he was in my village," Ord said.

"Ord only took about ten days to learn to speak our language," Bruna said.

Vistern scratched his chin and stared at Ord. "You obviously have a gift for languages like Bruna. Would you be willing to be my translator and travel with me to Egypt?"

"Will you pay me in gold?" Ord asked.

"Yes. I'll pay you five units of gold, but you will need to learn to speak Minoan and Egyptian."

"I will be your translator, and I'll soon learn the other two languages," Ord said.

Vistern pointed to a man sitting by the fire. "He'll be travelling with us. He's a Minoan and he'll teach you his language during our journey."

While Vistern talked to Bruna, Ord and Mud Face drank beer and ate the beef.

Ord did not like the beer, but the beef was delicious. Beef was his favourite meat. "We'll now be travelling to Egypt," he said to Mud Face.

Mud Face frowned. "Will we have to travel across the sea?"

"Yes, I think so."

Mud Face looked worried. "I don't like travelling across the sea. Do we have to go?"

"Yes. I've given my word. At least this time, I'll not have to walk and will be able to ride my horse. I can't wait to see the tombs that are several times bigger than tall trees."

"I've been riding your horse," Mud Face said. "If you ride your horse, I won't have a horse to ride."

"Will you provide a horse for Mud Face to ride, Vistern?" Ord asked.

Vistern nodded. "I'll provide a horse for her to ride. We'll be leaving at dawn."

"We'll be ready," Ord said.

*

At dawn, the caravan of travellers assembled in the centre of the village. There was Ord and Mud Face, Vistern and his woman, Haffa, the Minoan and six armed guards. There were also ten other travellers who would be travelling part of the way with them. They were all on horseback and loaded down with provisions. Mud Face had been given a small white horse to ride.

"Do you always have six guards to protect you, Vistern?" Ord asked.

"No. I usually have four guards. We need the extra two guards because we'll be taking a huge amount of gold and silver with us. This will be my last trip as a trader. I'll have more than enough wealth to last me for the rest of my life."

As soon as they set off, Ord rode near to the Minoan and began talking to him. He wanted to learn the Minoan language as soon as possible.

At the end of the day, they stopped, lit a fire and cooked a wild boar that the men had killed. The meat would last them for many days.

"I don't like Haffa," Mud Face said. "She's being very nasty to me."

Ord glanced at Haffa. She was plain-looking and had large breasts. "How is she being nasty to you?"

"She said that I'm not a woman because I don't have any breasts. I do have breasts, but they're still small. She said that men only like women with large breasts."

"Men do like women with large breasts," he said. "But don't worry, you'll soon have large breasts."

"She said that you will not want to have sex with me if I have small breasts."

"When you're ready to have sex, I'll have sex with you even if you have small breasts," he said. "Don't go near Haffa. Stay near me. She's Vistern's woman, and she can afford to be nasty." He did not like anyone being nasty to Mud Face and would one day find a way to repay Haffa in kind.

Ord and Mud Face sat down next to Vistern.

Vistern looked at Ord's bow. "Bruna said you're a very good bowman and can fight like ten men. He told me how you killed the four robbers."

"It was easy," Ord said. "They were poor bowmen. The gods were on my side."

"You believe in five gods," Vistern said.

"Yes. Everyone believes in five gods."

"They don't."

Ord was surprised. "I thought everyone believed in five gods."

"In your land, they believe in five gods," Vistern said. "There are many religions in the world, and they all have different gods to you."

"I didn't realise," Ord said. "I thought there was only one religion and that everyone worshipped our five gods."

"In parts of my land, they worship just three gods," Vistern said. "In other parts, they worship ten gods. The Minoans have many gods. Some of their gods are goddesses, and some are part animal and part man. One of their most important gods is the snake goddess."

Ord was amazed. "The Minoans worship female gods?"

"Yes. The Egyptians also worship gods that have animal heads, and when they die, they expect to become stars in the heavens."

Ord tried to imagine female gods and gods with animal heads. "They must be simple-minded people to have such foolish gods."

"They are not simple-minded. The Minoans and the Egyptians are the most intelligent people on earth. Do you have a strong belief in your five gods?"

"Yes. What gods do you believe in?"

Vistern looked into the flames of the fire. "I was brought up to believe in three gods. The sun god, the god of fertility and the god of our ancestors. After travelling all over the world and learning about many other gods, I now only believe in one god."

"What god is that?" Ord asked.

"The god of our ancestors. I believe that the spirits of our ancestors are the gods."

"Do you offer sacrifices to your ancestor gods?" Ord asked.

"No. I don't believe in sacrifices. They make no difference to what happens. Everyone gets old and dies and becomes ill at times, even if they make dozens of sacrifices to the gods. The sun will always rise in the mornings, and the summer will always follow the winter." He looked at Ord. "What would happen to me if I put a curse on your gods?"

"Something horrible."

"I've cursed all the gods I know about," Vistern said. "I've cursed them many times."

Ord was shocked. "And what happened?"

"Nothing." Vistern stood up and held his arms in the air. "Do you hear me, sun god?"

Everyone looked at the sun that was setting behind the trees.

"I don't believe that you have any power, sun god," Vistern said. "I don't believe you are a god. If you are a god, then do not rise in the morning or strike me dead. Come on, strike me dead."

No one spoke, and Ord held his breath. No one had ever mocked the gods before. He expected something terrible to happen to Vistern, but nothing happened.

Vistern sat down and drank some beer. "I've ridiculed all the Minoan gods and the Egyptian gods. They are all powerless. They are not gods."

Ord felt confused. He could not believe that someone could mock the sun god and not be killed. "I thought everyone was frightened of the gods."

"I'm not. They don't frighten me. Why should I believe that something is a god just because someone thinks it is a god?"

"If there are no gods, why do people believe in gods?" Ord asked.

"Because they are weak. People are filled with fear of the unknown. It makes them feel brave if they think that a god is protecting them. People are frightened of death and of becoming ill, and of evil spirits, and so they rely on gods to protect them. If they had any brains, they'd realise that their gods are powerless. The people who believe in gods still suffer and die."

Ord had a drink of beer. "I've always believed in the gods. I find it difficult to believe that you don't believe in any of the gods."

"I suppose we all need something to believe in," Vistern said. "I still believe in the spirits of our ancestors. The only good thing about religion and belief in gods is that it unites people. Leaders use religion to control men so that they can get them to do what they want."

"I'm frightened that the sun will not rise up tomorrow," Mud Face whispered.

Vistern laughed. "There's no need to worry, Mud Face. The sun will always rise up in the mornings." He turned to look at Ord. "It's very important that you pretend to believe in the gods of the people we visit. You must always show respect for their gods."

"I will," Ord said. Darkness was descending on them, and he felt nervous. He took a long drink of beer. If the sun did not rise in the morning, he would know who to blame.

Ord and Mud Face lay down together with Dip under a tree.

"I feel frightened," Mud Face said. "If there are no gods, who will protect us?"

"I will protect us," Ord said. He put his arm around her shoulders. "I'm big and strong." He was acting braver than he felt.

*

Ord woke up. Mud Face was shaking his arm. "Get up," she said. "Get up, Ord."

He sat up and grabbed his bow. "What's wrong?"

"There's nothing wrong." She pointed at the brightening sky. "Look."

He rubbed the sleep from his eyes and looked up at the sky. It was dawn. He began to stroke Dip. "What am I supposed to be looking at?"

"The sky. It's getting light."

He could not understand what she was talking about. "The sky always gets light at dawn."

"I was frightened that we would never see the sun again after what Vistern did," she said.

"Oh, yes." He stood up. "It looks as if the sun is rising as Vistern said it would." He looked at Vistern, who was urinating over a bush. "And Vistern looks healthy and has not been struck dead."

Mudd Face frowned. "I don't understand. If the sun is a powerful god, why didn't he kill Vistern?"

Ord chewed his lip. "I don't know. It's very strange. Maybe Vistern is right, and there are no gods, just the spirits of the dead."

"Do you think the spirits of the dead protect us?" she asked.

"I don't know. Maybe they do."

"The spirit of my grandmother would protect us if she could," she said.

He kissed her on the nose. "Then we have no need to worry. With the spirit of your grandmother to protect us, nothing will harm us. Let's get something to eat."

During the journey, a woman belonging to one of the men who was travelling with them died. They continued the journey and just left the dead body by the side of the road for the wild animals to eat.

"Why didn't they cremate that dead woman?" Mud Face asked Ord.

"Not everyone's cremated," Ord said. "Most poor people, when they die, are left out in the open for animals to eat. Many years ago, everyone was left out in the open when they died. Now, important people are cremated."

Vistern, who had overheard them talking, said, "Things are now changing. Up to now, all important people were cremated, and their ashes were buried in holy ground inside the circle made by the ditch and a mound. Now, some important people are not being cremated, and their bodies are being buried in burial mounds with some of their possessions."

"Are you going to be cremated or buried, Vistern?" Ord asked.

Vistern smiled. "I'm not going to die. I'm going to live forever."

While they were setting up camp for the night, one of the men travelling with them began talking to Mud Face. He was a big, mean-looking man.

When Ord was sitting by the fire with Mud Face, he asked, "What did that man say to you, Mud Face?"

"He wanted me to be his woman. I told him I was your woman. I don't like him. He frightens me."

"Don't worry, I'll protect you," Ord said. "He will not harm you."

Vistern sat down next to Ord and Mud Face.

"There could be trouble," Vistern said.

"What trouble?" Ord asked.

"I've been talking to Saydan and his brother Pundeb. It was their woman who died, and they want Mud Face to be their woman. They always share the same woman for sex."

"Mud Face is my woman," Ord said. "I don't share Mud Face with anyone."

"It would be better to let them have Mud Face," Vistern said. "A woman's not worth dying for. The two brothers and their two guards are the meanest fighting men I've ever seen. The big man is Saydan. I've seen him kill a man with his bare hands. If you try to stop them taking Mud Face, they will kill you."

Mud Face looked terrified. "I don't want to be their woman. I'm your woman, Ord."

"Don't worry, Mud Face," Ord said. "No one's going to take you. There are seven of us, and only four of them. They would be foolish to attack us."

"If you fight them, you will be on your own," Vistern said. "My men will not be helping you. My advice is to let them take Mud Face."

Ord was angry that Vistern would not be helping him. He would remember this betrayal.

The two brothers and their two guards walked towards them.

Ord stood up and put an arrow to his bow. He pointed. "Go and stand behind that tree, Mud Face. I don't want you getting hurt."

Mud Face ran and hid behind the tree.

The four men stopped on the other side of the fire and stared at Ord. They each had an arrow to their bow.

"I'm Saydan," the big man said.

Vistern stood up. "Ord will not give you his woman, Saydan. You can get a woman from the next village. A woman's not worth fighting over."

"I want Mud Face," Saydan said.

"You will not be having Mud Face," Ord said. "She's my woman."

"If you don't give me Mud Face, I will kill you," Saydan said.

"Then you will have to kill me," Ord said.

"A woman's not worth dying for," Saydan said. "Vistern's told me that his men will not be fighting with you. You're just one man against four. We will not harm you if you give us Mud Face." He smiled. "I would hate to deprive Vistern of his translator."

"To take Mud Face, you will first have to kill me," Ord said. "No one touches my women."

"You're a fool, Ord," Vistern said.

Vistern and his six guards walked away from the fire.

“Give us Mud Face, or you die,” Saydan shouted.

Before Saydan’s booming voice had faded away, Ord had shot him in the throat. Ord then shot each one of the men in the throat. They were all standing about six paces from him, so it was easy to hit their throats. They were extremely fast and accurate with the bow, and Ord was hit three times in the chest by arrows. Ord jumped over the fire as the four men writhed on the ground and cut their throats with his flint knife.

Mud Face ran up to Ord. “You’ve been shot three times,” she cried. “Oh, no. Are you in pain?”

“Yes,” Ord said. He pulled the arrows out of his armour.”

“No man can live when he’s been shot three times,” Mud Face said, and tears began to run down her face. “You’re going to die, and it was my fault.”

“It was not your fault,” Ord said. “You’re my woman, and you will always be my woman.”

Vistern walked up to Ord. “You’re unbelievably fast and accurate with a bow, but fighting them has cost you your life.”

“I’m not so sure,” Ord said. It was now time to see if his armour had worked. He took off his armour and his tunic and examined his wounds. Each arrow had made a small hole in his chest, but none of the arrowheads had gone into his chest. “I think I’ll live.”

Everyone gathered around Ord and examined his wounds.

“There must have been something wrong with their arrows; otherwise, you would be dead or dying,” Vistern said.

“I was saved by my armour,” Ord said.

Mud Face looked shocked. “How does your armour work?”

“It’s three layers of thick hide,” Ord said. “I’ve tested it, and it will stop an arrow from going into my chest.”

Vistern examined the arrows that had hit Ord. “There’s nothing wrong with the arrows. They’re very sharp.”

“Let me lick your wounds, Ord,” Mud Face said.

Ord frowned. “Why?”

“It cleans the wounds,” Mud Face said.

As Mud Face licked his wounds, he grimaced. The area around each wound was very bruised. “Be careful, Mud Face.”

She finished licking his wounds and looked up at him. “My grandmother said that licking a wound will stop it from getting infected.”

Ord put his tunic and armour back on and walked over to the four dead men. “Their four horses and their possessions are now mine,” he said. He took their bows and arrows and flint knives and put them into a saddlebag on his horse. He then walked over to the four horses he now owned and sorted through the possessions of the dead men that were inside their saddlebags. He was amazed to find a huge amount of gold, silver and jewellery in the saddlebags. Without telling the others about the gold, silver and jewellery, he put them into a saddlebag on his horse. He was now a very wealthy man.

"What will you do with the four horses, Ord?" Mud Face asked.

"I'll sell them. We cannot take them to Egypt."

Ord and Mud Face sat down by the fire.

"I'm glad you were wearing your armour," Mud Face said. "It saved your life."

"I didn't realise how good you were with a bow, Ord," Vistern said. "You're the quickest man I've ever seen and the most accurate."

"It would have been easier if your men had helped me," Ord said.

"I cannot risk my men fighting other people's battles, even your battles. I can manage without a translator, but I cannot manage without my guards."

"I don't think they would have attacked me if they'd known that your men would be fighting with me."

Vistern shrugged. "You could be right. Were they carrying any gold?"

"No. Just a flint axe and a flint knife."

"You will be able to sell the four horses in the next village we visit," Vistern said. "You'll get four units of gold for each horse."

When it was time to sleep, Ord took the saddlebag containing the gold and silver off his horse and lay down with Mud Face and Dip.

"I didn't find just a flint axe and a flint knife in the possessions of the two brothers," he whispered. "I also found a large amount of gold, gold necklaces, gold bracelets and gold rings."

Mud Face looked shocked. "You're now a very wealthy man."

"Yes, but I don't trust Vistern. If he discovers that I have gold, he will find some way to take it from me. If you see anyone go near my horse during the day, tell me."

"I will. They won't be able to steal it when we're asleep. Dip will warn us if anyone comes near us."

"I know." He was pleased that he had Dip with him.

Chapter eight

They could travel very fast on horseback, and it took them only eight days to reach the sea. Ord could now speak Minoan fluently. He had sold the four horses for four units of gold each at a village they passed on the way. When he walked into the village by the sea, he was amazed at the size of the village and the harbour. There were over forty huts. Two of the huts were large and were made of stone. What shocked him the most was the size of the boats moored in the harbour. They were over fifteen paces long and ten paces wide. He watched one of the boats leave the harbour and sail out to sea. It had two huge sails that filled with wind and pushed the boat along.

"I didn't realise that they could make boats that big," Mud Face said. "Are we going to sail on the sea on one of those?"

"I think so," Ord said. "Let's get something to eat."

They sat down by the fire with Vistern and Haffa. It was late in the afternoon.

"The other travellers have a different destination and will be leaving us today," Vistern said. "We'll be travelling by sea to the land of the Minoans. How are you getting on with the Minoan language?"

"I can speak the language now," Ord said.

Vistern looked at the Minoan and then back at Ord. "You've learnt to speak Minoan in eight days?"

"Yes."

"It would take me six years to learn to speak a foreign language," Vistern said. "How is it you can learn a language so quickly? What do you do?"

"I just remember what the words mean," Ord said. "Once you learn the basic words, it becomes easy."

"After we've traded with the Minoans, we'll be trading with the Egyptians and going to their city of stone, and you will need to learn how to speak Egyptian."

"That won't be a problem," Ord said. "Will we be seeing the massive tombs of the pharaohs?"

"I think so. Just remember to show them and their gods great respect. The Minoans are easy-going, but the Egyptians can be very unpredictable and very violent."

"I will."

After eating, Ord, Mud Face and Dip settled down to sleep by their horses. Ord slept with his head resting on the saddlebag containing his possessions and with Dip by his side.

*

At dawn, they loaded the horses and their provisions onto one of the large sea boats and climbed aboard. The horses were tied up in standing positions with hay to eat. Ord sat down next to Mud Face, Vistern, Haffa and Dip. There was water in the bottom of the boat.

"Will we have to bail out the water?" Ord asked Vistern.

"No. My guards will do that. They'll also help row the boat if the wind fails."

The wind was strong, and it filled the sails, and the boat sailed out to sea.

Mud Face held Ord's arm. "I don't like being on a boat," she said. "I don't like going up and down. The waves are very big."

"How far will we be travelling at sea, Vistern?" Ord asked.

"All the way to the land of the Minoans. It will take about four days. It depends on the wind. We'll only be travelling at sea during the day. Each evening, we'll pull into a harbour. It's too dangerous to sail the sea at night."

"I think Mud Face is frightened," Haffa said. "I think she's a baby."

Vistern smiled.

"I'm also frightened, Haffa," Ord said. "Do you think I'm a baby?"

Haffa smiled. "If you're frightened of sailing on a boat, then you must be a baby. Are you frightened that the boat might sink?"

"I'm surprised that a man as powerful as you would have a woman like Haffa, Vistern," Ord said.

Vistern looked at Haffa. "She's not too bad."

"She's a pain in the neck and would drive me mad," Ord said.

"You're jealous because I have huge breasts, and Mud Face doesn't have any," Haffa said. She pulled out her breasts and bounced them up and down. "I bet you'd do anything to get your hands on these."

Ord looked at her breasts. "You do have large breasts, and the reason why you're always showing them off is so that the men won't look at your face. If they did, they would quickly lose interest in you."

Haffa put her breasts away. "I'm also pretty."

"Pretty ugly," Ord said. "You're the one who's jealous, Haffa. You're jealous of Mud Face's beauty. She's the most beautiful woman who has ever lived."

"I wish Bruna was here," Haffa said. "He was a much nicer person than you, Ord."

Ord ignored her and looked away. It would be better if he did not talk to her.

The journey was nerve-racking, and the waves were almost coming into the boat. Ord was frightened that the boat would sink, although he kept his fear hidden. Vistern's six bodyguards had to bail out the water continually.

Mud Face was holding onto Ord's arm. "I feel sick."

"So do I," Ord said. "I always feel sick when I'm on a boat."

Mud Face looked at Haffa. "I'm frightened, and I don't care who knows it."

"I'm also frightened," Ord said. "I'd feel better if I could swim."

"I don't think people can swim," Mud Face said.

"People can swim," Vistern said. "It's supposed to be easy to learn to swim, although I've never tried to."

"Can we learn to swim, Ord?" Mud Face asked.

"Yes," Ord said. He might not feel so sick if he could swim.

When night began to fall, they sailed into a harbour.

Ord would be glad to get his feet onto solid ground. "I like travelling but not sailing," he said to Mud Face.

"I don't like sailing or travelling," Mud Face said. "I won't be happy until we're back in our village."

They all climbed off the boat and sat down by a fire to eat.

"Have you noticed anything strange about the six guards?" Mud Face whispered to Ord.

Ord looked at the six men, who were laughing at something. "No. They look normal enough to me."

"I think they are men who lie with men," Mud Face said. "They always lie down together at night, like we do."

"I hadn't noticed," Ord said. He could not understand why a man would like a man in a sexual way.

"You're a very unusual man, Ord," Vistern said.

"Why am I unusual?"

"You're different to other men. I think that one day you will be a leader of men."

"Why do you think that?"

"You're very big and strong and clever. Very few men can learn to speak a new language in a few days. You're also a very good bowman. What will make you a leader of men is your bravery. You didn't show any fear when you fought the two brothers and their two guards. Most men would have been frightened. Did you feel any fear?"

"No. I just do what has to be done."

"I think you're very brave, Ord," Mud Face whispered.

*

It took them four days to reach the land of the Minoans, and they sailed into a huge harbour as the day was ending. Ord was spellbound. He had never seen anything like it before. Most of the buildings he could see were huge and made of stone, and several of the boats that were moored in the harbour were twice as big as the boat he was on.

"What sort of place is this, Vistern?" Ord asked.

"It's one of the many Minoan stone cities. Everything's made of stone or bricks, even the homes. I'll be trading with the Minoans, and you will be needed to translate for me. I'll be trading gold for some fantastically carved gold objects. The Minoans are the most talented workers in metal."

After the horses had been taken off the boat, they walked to one of the few wooden buildings.

"We'll be spending the night in this building," Vistern said. "At dawn, we'll be travelling north to another stone city to do the trading."

A young woman walked up to them. "I'm one of the temple maidens," she said. "Do you want the services of a beautiful young maiden for a very small price?"

"What did she say?" Vistern asked.

"I think she's asking if we want to have sex with a young woman," Ord said. "She says she's a temple maiden."

"She's a prostitute," Vistern said. "They sell their bodies for sex. Tell her that we're not interested."

"We don't want the services of your beautiful maidens," Ord said to the woman.

The young woman smiled and walked away.

"I didn't realise that women sold their bodies for money," Mud Face said. "What sort of husbands do they have?"

"They're not married," Vistern said. "This land and Egypt are full of prostitutes. If you have sex with one of them, you're bound to catch a sexually transmitted disease. The men and women I've seen with these diseases die a terrible death."

"I don't know much about sexually transmitted diseases," Ord said.

"As long as you don't pay to have sex with a prostitute, you'll be safe," Vistern said. "And keep well away from beggars. Some of them also carry diseases that you can catch. There's one disease that makes your fingers and toes fall off."

“I wouldn’t like to catch that disease,” Mud Face said.

They did not light a fire and sat down to a meal of bread and cold meat.

The more Ord discovered about his world, the more amazed he became. He had never dreamed that boats could be so large, that cities could be made of stone, and that woman sold their bodies for sex. What amazed him the most was that the people who could make huge boats and build cities of stone worshipped a female god.

Vistern had watched Ord take the saddlebag containing his gold off his horse and lie down with it next to Mud Face and Dip. Vistern was a clever man, and he had probably already guessed that the two brothers that Ord had killed had been carrying gold. Ord was beginning to get to know Vistern, and he expected him to try to steal his gold.

*

At dawn, they led their horses and walked through the city of stone.

Ord was amazed by the size of the stone temples and buildings. “How do they manage to build such large buildings, Vistern?” Ord asked.

“I don’t know. It must have taken them many years.”

“And these people worship a female snake goddess?” Ord said.

Vistern nodded. “Yes. They are very strange people.”

Mud Face held onto Ord’s arm as they led their horses along a road surrounded on each side by tall buildings and people selling all manner of foods and goods. “If we told the people in our village about this city of stone, they would not believe us,” she said.

They left the city, climbed onto their horses and rode to the other city of stone.

Ord had been intimidated by the large buildings, and he felt more relaxed in the countryside. “How far do we have to go, Vistern?”

“Only for a short distance,” Vistern said. “When we reach the top of this hill, you’ll see that we’re on a large island.”

They reached the top of the hill, and Ord admired the view. He could see the entire large island they were on, and far out to sea. He could also see the city of stone they were heading for. Even though he hated sailing on the sea, he appreciated the opportunity he had been given to see the world.

They reached the other city of stone, entered a large building and Ord, Vistern, and an old man sat down in front of a table. Vistern handed a skin with drawings on it to the old man.

“Ask him if he still has these items for sale?” Vistern said.

“Do you still have these items for sale?” Ord asked the old man in Minoan.

The old man looked at the drawings. “Yes. We still have them for sale.”

"He still has all the items for sale," Ord said to Vistern.

"Ask him if I can see them?" Vistern said.

"Can we see them?" Ord asked the old man.

The old man nodded and stood up. "I'll go and get them." He walked out of the room.

"Are you buying these things for yourself or for other people?" Ord asked Vistern.

"The gold ring is for me, but the other items are for several wealthy leaders of the tribes in my land."

The old man returned with a large leather bag and placed it on the table. "These items are beautiful works of art."

"He said that they're beautiful works of art," Ord said to Vistern.

Vistern carefully examined the finely decorated gold rings, broaches, pendants, necklaces, bracelets and a gold beaker. Ord had never seen anything so beautiful in his life.

"Ask him how much gold he wants for them?" Vistern said.

"The trader wants to know how much gold you want for them?" Ord asked the old man.

"For all of them, I would want eight hundred units of gold," the old man said.

"He wants eight hundred units of gold," Ord said to Vistern.

Vistern shook his head. "That's too much. He told me last year that he wanted five hundred units of gold. Tell him that I'll give him five hundred units of gold."

Ord told the old man what Vistern had said, but the old man refused to accept it. Ord translated what they said, and the bartering lasted for some time. Eventually, they agreed on six hundred units of gold.

They both used their own weighing machines to weigh the gold. It was a huge amount of gold. There was a slight discrepancy between the weighing machines, but they eventually agreed on the amount, and Vistern and Ord left with the gold items.

"What are we going to do now?" Ord asked Vistern.

"We're going to travel back to the other city of stone and then sail to Egypt. There's very little silver mined in Egypt, and they're willing to exchange gold for silver. We'll then return here, and I'll purchase a few more gold items."

They rode back to the other city of stone, where the large boats were moored in the harbour, and tied their horses up outside the wooden hut where they had slept before.

Ord took the saddlebag containing his gold off his horse.

“My men will guard the horses and your possessions, Ord,” Vistern said.

Ord glanced at the six guards. “I don’t trust them. They didn’t protect me when I was attacked by the two brothers and their two guards.”

“They will protect you and your possessions now,” Vistern said. “You can leave your saddlebag on your horse.”

“I would rather guard the few possessions I have,” Ord said. “The flint knives and axes that the brothers had are of good quality.”

“Show them to me,” Vistern said.

“Why?”

“I think that your saddlebag also contains some gold. I think the brothers were carrying gold.”

Ord smiled. It would be pointless trying to fool a man like Vistern. “You’re right. I’m now the owner of two gold rings and a gold bracelet, and the gold I got for selling the four horses. I’m now a rich man.”

Vistern smiled. “Not as rich as me.”

“Not yet, Vistern, but one day I might be.”

Ord lay down with Mud Face and Dip and his saddlebag containing his possessions.

“I thought you had a large amount of gold,” Mud Face whispered.

“I do. I lied to Vistern.”

“What will you do if Vistern wants to look into your saddlebag?” Mud Face whispered. “He probably suspects that you have a large amount of gold.”

“He probably does, but I’ll refuse to show him my gold. If he knows I have a large amount of gold, he will definitely try to take it from me.”

“Will you fight Vistern’s six guards for your gold?” Mud Face asked.

“Yes, if I have to. No one’s going to have my gold.”

Chapter Nine

In the morning, Ord picked up his saddlebag and walked out of the hut. It was raining. The sky was covered in grey clouds, and the waves on the sea were very large. When they approached the owners of the boats, they were told that no boats would be sailing until the storm had passed. Ord was pleased; it would give him and Mud Face the opportunity to learn how to swim.

Ord, Mud Face and Dip walked down to the shore and found a protected cove. There was no one about. He tied his saddlebag to Dip and took off his clothes.

"What are you doing? Ord?" Mud Face asked. When they were alone, they always spoke in their native language.

"I'm going to learn how to swim. Take off your clothes and join me."

She looked about. "Someone might come. I don't want to be seen naked."

"If someone comes, we can put our clothes back on."

He walked into the sea. If he could learn a foreign language in ten days, he would find it easy to learn to swim.

"Is the water cold?" she asked.

"No. It's much warmer than the river water in our land. Come on in."

She took off her clothes, waded into the sea and stood next to him. "What do we have to do to swim?"

"When we first arrived at this island, I watched young children swimming in the sea. They just threw themselves into the sea and waved their hands about and kicked their feet."

"Is that what you're going to do?" she asked.

"Yes. It looks easy to do."

He lowered himself into the water and thrashed about with his arms. Instead of swimming, he sank below the water. He stood up and wiped the water from his face.

She began to laugh. "You're supposed to stay above the water, not sink below it."

"I know. It's not as easy as I thought. You have a go and see if you can swim."

She lowered herself into the water and moved her arms about. "Is this swimming?"

He smiled. "No. You're still standing on the bottom. Lift your feet up and kick them in the water."

She lifted her feet off the bottom and sank below the waves.

He lifted her out of the water. "You have to move your arms about as well."

She wiped the water from her face. "It's very difficult. You try."

"I can't understand why it's so easy for little children to swim," he said. He lifted his feet from the bottom, kicked them and thrashed his arms about, but he still sank below the waves. He stood up and wiped the water from his face.

"I don't think you're doing it right," she said.

"I'll soon get the hang of it," he said.

Each time he tried to swim and failed, she laughed. It was very frustrating.

He stood waist-deep in the sea, watching her laugh. She was beautiful beyond belief. "Are you going to have another go?" he asked.

"No. Once was enough. I'll just watch you." She waded out of the sea and got dressed.

"I must be doing something wrong," he said.

She sat on a rock and put her head in her hands. "If you can't swim, I don't think I'll ever be able to swim."

Ord tried several more times to swim and then gave up and got dressed. "I didn't realise it would be so difficult to learn to swim. We'll just have to hope that the boats we sail on don't sink."

They walked back to Vistern and his guards, who were sitting outside the wooden hut.

Vistern stood up. "Where have you been, Ord?"

"Down to the sea."

"Why?" Vistern asked.

"I wanted to learn how to swim."

"Did you manage to swim?" Vistern asked.

"No. I'm good at sinking but not at swimming."

"I want you to learn how to speak Egyptian," Vistern said. "While we're waiting for the storm to pass, go into the city and try to find someone who will be willing to teach you to speak Egyptian."

"I'll find someone," Ord said.

Ord, Mud Face and Dip walked into the City.

"How are you going to find someone to teach you to speak Egyptian?" Mud Face asked.

"I don't know. I'll ask some of the people in the market."

Ord spoke to a few people, but no one spoke Egyptian. It was going to be more difficult than he had thought.

As they walked past a large temple, a beggar boy aged about ten walked up to them. "Give food, please?" he asked.

"What did he say?" Mud Face asked.

"He's a beggar, and he wants some food."

"We don't have any food," Ord said to the boy.

"He looks hungry," Mud Face said. "Ask him if he speaks Egyptian?"

"I don't think so," Ord said. "He can hardly speak Minoan."

"Do you speak Egyptian?" Ord asked the boy.

The boy nodded. "Yes. I born in Egypt. I speak Egyptian."

"What did he say?" Mud Face asked.

"He said that he can speak Egyptian."

"Ask him if he'll teach you to speak Egyptian," Mud Face said.

"Do you want to work for me?" Ord asked the boy.

The boy nodded. "Yes. Yes. I work for you. What work I do?"

"I want you to teach me to speak Egyptian," Ord said. "If you do, I'll feed you."

While nodding his head, the boy said, "I work for you. I teach you Egyptian."

What's your name?" Ord asked.

"My name's Sud."

"My name's Ord. This is my wife, Mud Face, and this is Dip, my dog. Come with us."

The three of them and Dip walked back to Vistern, who was sitting outside the hut, eating.

"I've found someone to teach me to speak Egyptian," Ord said. "He's a beggar. His name's Sud. All we have to do is feed him."

"Good," Vistern said. "Start learning Egyptian now."

Ord gave Sud some bread and fish. When he had eaten the food, they walked down to the beach and sat on some rocks.

"What is the Egyptian word for man, Sud?" Ord asked.

"What did you say, Ord?" Mud Face asked. "I don't like not understanding you."

"I was asking him the Egyptian word for man," Ord said. "When he tells me what man is in Egyptian, you can tell him what man is in our language. Sud will then learn to speak our language."

*

They had to wait seven days for the storms to pass. During this time, Ord learned to speak Egyptian, and Mud Face taught Sud to speak their native language. Sud was very good at learning a new language, and he was now able to communicate with Ord and Mud Face. When the three of them were alone together, they always spoke in Ord's native tongue.

"We'll be going to Egypt tomorrow, Ord," Vistern said. "Can you speak Egyptian yet?"

"Yes."

Vistern frowned. "How well can you speak Egyptian?"

"Reasonably well."

"I don't know how you do it," Vistern said. "Tell Sud to go. We don't need him anymore."

"I want him to stay with us," Ord said.

Vistern looked surprised. "Why?"

"He doesn't have a family, and I feel sorry for him."

"What's he going to do if he stays with us?" Vistern asked.

"I promised him a job."

"And what job will that be?"

"He can be my servant."

"You don't need a servant, Ord," Haffa said. "You're being foolish. Don't expect Vistern to pay for Sud's food so that he can be your servant."

"I'll pay for his food while he travels with us," Ord said.

"You're a fool, Ord," Vistern said. "These beggars are thieves and cannot be trusted. If he comes with us, I'll hold you responsible for any thieving he does."

"He's not a thief," Ord said.

"If you insist on having Sud as your servant while you're with me, it'll cost you one unit of gold," Vistern said.

"That's a very high price," Ord said.

Vistern shrugged. "Take it or leave it."

Ord gave Vistern a unit of gold. The more he knew about Vistern, the less he liked him.

Ord, Mud Face, Sud and Dip sat down a short distance from Vistern and Haffa.

"Am I your servant now?" Sud asked Ord. He was speaking in Ord's native tongue.

"Yes."

"What will I have to do?" Sud asked.

"I don't know yet," Ord said. "I'll think of something. Do you steal things?"

"Yes," Sud said. "I had to steal to survive."

"From now on, you will not steal anything, Sud," Ord said.

"I only stole food because I was hungry," Sud said. "Thanks for making me your servant. Will I be going back with you to your land?"

"Yes," Ord said.

"Where is it?" Sud asked.

"It's a long way from here, across the sea," Mud Face said. "You will be able to help me look after the animals. I wonder what the people in our village are doing now?"

"Probably walking through the snow," Ord said."

She frowned. "Why do you think that?"

"It's now winter in our land, and there's probably snow on the ground."

"I don't like the snow," she said.

"What is snow?" Sud asked. "Is it like mud?"

"No," Mud Face said. "It's white and cold." She frowned. "How would you explain snow, Ord?"

"I don't know. You'll have to wait and see it for yourself, Sud."

Sud began to play with Dip.

"If you had not given Sud a job, he would have probably starved to death," Mud Face said. She looked up at him. "I'm glad you saved him. I'm also glad that we're now having sex. Are you glad that we're now having sex?"

"Yes."

"Do you like having sex with me?" she asked.

He smiled. "Yes."

"My breasts are beginning to grow, and I'll soon be a proper woman."

"You're already a proper woman," he said. "You have a beautiful figure and a beautiful face."

"Are you just saying that to be nice?" she asked.

"No. Isn't Mud Face beautiful, Sud?"

"Yes. She's very beautiful. Am I beautiful?"

Mud Face punched Sud on the arm. "No. Men are not supposed to be beautiful."

*

They set sail for Egypt at dawn. It was a warm, windy day. This time, they were sailing on the biggest boat Ord had ever seen. It was at least forty paces long and twenty paces wide. There were twelve horses on board, fifteen people, and a large number of bags and large jugs. The wind was strong, and it not only filled the three sails but also produced large waves. At times, it was frightening. Thanks to the wind, it took them just one day to reach Egypt. The harbour they sailed into was even bigger than the Minoan harbour.

They led their horses off the boat and rode through the city. Sud rode with Mud Face on her horse. The city of stone was very intimidating. Some of the buildings were twice as tall as a large tree.

"Where are we going, Vistern?" Ord asked.

"To another city of stone. It's a three-day ride away."

"Are these huge buildings temples?" Ord asked.

"Yes. The Egyptians build more temples and statues than anyone else. If we're stopped by armed Egyptians, be very friendly. Do not upset them. Just tell them that we're here to trade with the pharaoh."

"I will," Ord said.

"How do you feel being back in the land of your birth, Sud?" Mud Face asked. When she spoke to Sud, she spoke in her native tongue.

"It's strange," Sud said. "I don't remember much about Egypt. I was only seven when I left to go to the land of the Minoans."

Mud Face looked about as they rode along. "These people are very different to us, Ord. They're almost naked, and the men have smooth faces, and some of them are completely bald."

"I know," Ord said. "They look very strange."

"They shave their faces and heads with very sharp flint knives," Vistern said.

Ord could not believe his eyes. Several men were riding by on the strangest horses he had ever seen. "What sort of creatures are those?"

Vistern smiled. "They're camels. This land is full of strange creatures."

"And strange trees," Mud Face said. She pointed. "I've never seen trees like them. This is a very strange land."

When they stopped for the night, Ord, Mud Face and Sud were given some strange food to eat.

"What sort of food is this, Sud?" Ord asked.

"It's a food called dates," Sud said. He held up another strange-looking food. "This is a fig. They're quite nice to eat."

That night, they slept beneath the stars. As usual, Ord, Mud Face, Sud and Dip slept together.

*

After three days of travelling, they rode to meet the man Vistern intended to trade with. It was warm and Ord would like to take his armour off, but he decided to keep it on. It was better to be hot and sweaty than dead. When they reached the small city of stone, they were told that the man they needed to see was not there but would be returning in a few days. Ord had no problem speaking Egyptian and translating for Vistern.

"Where are the large tombs, Vistern?" Ord asked.

Vistern pointed. "About a day's ride in that direction."

"I'd like to see them," Ord said.

"It's too late to go now. The sun is about to set. You'll have to go at dawn. Go straight there and back. You won't get lost if you keep to the main road."

"Are they easy to find?" Ord asked.

Vistern smiled. "The tombs are as big as mountains. You will not be able to miss them. The Egyptians call them pyramids."

"Will I be going with you, Ord?" Mud Face asked.

"Yes, and Sud and Dip. How can I protect you, Mud Face, if you're not with me?"

She smiled.

*

At dawn, Ord, Mud Face and Sud rode off to see the large pyramids with Dip running on ahead.

"Have you seen the pyramids, Sud?" Ord asked.

"Yes."

"What are they like?" Mud Face asked Sud.

"They're very big. I was only about six when I saw them."

Ord was enjoying his adventure but was now eager to return to his land. He could now speak four languages, knew how to barter, and he had a good idea what gold items were worth, but his desire to be a trader was beginning to fade. It was a very dangerous occupation. He would see how he felt when he got home.

At the end of the day, they caught sight of the large pyramids in the distance.

"They do look big," Ord said.

"It's difficult to say how big they are from this distance," Mud Face said.

The sun was setting when they reached the pyramids. Ord sat on his horse, looking up at them with his mouth open. He could not believe what he was seeing. "It's impossible for men to build tombs so big."

"They frighten me," Mud Face said. "Is there a dead pharaoh inside each pyramid, Sud?"

"I think so," Sud said. "I don't know much about pyramids."

People were travelling to and fro. Most were walking, but some were riding horses and camels. They looked at Ord, Mud Face and Sud but did not speak.

They spent the night sleeping next to a huge statue of a dog with the head of a man. It was a cloudless night, and the heavens were full of stars.

"The Egyptians believe that when they die, they change into one of the stars," Ord said.

"Only important people and pharaohs become stars," Sud said.

She looked up. "It must be boring being a star. I wouldn't like to spend forever stuck in the sky. I'd much rather be on earth."

"So would I," Ord said.

*

At dawn, they rode right up to the largest pyramid. It was made of large square stones.

"How did men carry the large stones to the top?" Mud Face asked Sud.

"I don't know." He looked at Ord. "How did they carry the stones to the top?"

"I don't know. What I would like to know is why they built them in the first place. A tomb, even for a very important man, does not have to be that big."

"The Egyptians are very strange people," Mud Face said. "Let's go back to Vistern. I don't like being here."

"I don't either, although I'm glad I saw them," Ord said.

They began to ride back along the road towards the city of stone, where Vistern was. It was like being in another world. The trees were different; the buildings were different; the animals were different; the people were different; everything was different.

"Do you still want to be a trader, Ord?" Mud Face asked.

"I don't know. I know how to be a trader, and I can speak the languages. What I don't like is sailing across the seas."

"When we get home, I'll be having children, and I won't be able to go with you," she said. "I don't want you to be a trader. With all the gold you have, you'll be a wealthy man, and you'll be able to buy lots of animals and land."

"Do you have a lot of gold, Ord?" Sud asked.

"Yes, but don't tell anyone, especially Vistern."

"I won't," Sud said.

"If I'm not going to be a trader, I'll breed horses," Ord said. "I could make a good living breeding horses."

"We can help you, can't we, Sud?" Mud Face said.

Sud nodded.

*

The day was ending when Ord, Mud Face and Sud met up with Vistern and they sat down with him for a meal of strange food.

"Did you see the pyramids?" Vistern asked.

"Yes," Ord said. "I didn't think they would be so big. Even with hundreds of men, it must have taken many years to build them. We also saw the statue of a large dog with the head of a man."

"They call that a sphinx," Vistern said. "And it's not a dog. The animal is a lion. A lion is a very ferocious wild animal and is as big as a bull."

"I don't like this country," Mud Face said. "It's full of strange things."

"It's because you're a child, Mud Face," Haffa said. "You need to grow up."

Ord ignored her. "When we leave here, where will we be going, Vistern?"

"Back to see the old Minoan trader," Vistern said. "I want to get this large golden statue of an animal called an elephant. Last year, he told me that he wanted three hundred cubits of gold for the elephant. I'll just have enough when I've traded my silver for gold."

"Will we then be going back to your village?" Ord asked.

"Yes."

Ord, Mud Face, Sud and Dip spent the night sleeping under the stars next to the horses. As usual, Ord slept with his head resting on the saddlebag containing his possessions. Vistern kept looking at Ord's saddlebag, and it made Ord feel uneasy, which was why he always slept holding his bow.

*

The Egyptian trader had arrived during the night, and in the morning, Ord, Vistern and the Egyptian trader sat down together. Vistern placed a huge amount of silver in front of the trader.

"Tell him that I want to exchange this silver for the same weight in gold," Vistern said. "It weighs four hundred cubits."

"We want to trade this silver for the same weight in gold," Ord said to the trader. "It weighs four hundred cubits."

"I agree to the trade," the trader said. "We will weigh the silver."

"He agrees to the trade and wants to weigh the silver," Ord said to Vistern.

Vistern nodded.

They weighed the gold and the silver on a large weighing machine, and Vistern put the gold in the saddlebag on his horse. "That's the best trade I've ever done," he said. "They must be mad to trade silver for gold."

They had just started their journey back to the city of stone, where the harbour was, when they were approached by ten armed men on horses and a man on a two-wheeled cart pulled by a horse. The man, who was standing up on the cart, had a shaven head and was wearing a large golden necklace, a long white tunic and an animal skin over his shoulders.

"What sort of cart is that, Vistern?" Ord asks.

"It's a chariot. The man on the chariot is a very important man."

"Is he the pharaoh?" Ord asked.

"No. The pharaoh would have more men with him. He's a priest. Be very careful what you say. You must not upset this man."

The chariot pulled up in front of them.

"Who are you?" the man on the chariot asked.

Ord put an arrow to his bow. He wanted to be ready if trouble started. "We're traders."

"What did he say?" Vistern asked Ord.

"He wanted to know who we are," Ord said. "I told him that we were traders."

The man on the chariot pointed at Mud Face. "You. Get off your horse and come here."

Mud Face looked terrified. "Why is he pointing at me, Ord? What did he say?"

"Stay where you are, Mud Face," Ord said.

"What's going on, Ord?" Vistern asked.

"Why do you want that woman to get off her horse?" Ord asked the man on the chariot. "I'm the only one who can speak your language. We don't want any trouble. We just want to travel back to our land."

The man on the chariot looked at Ord. "Are you the translator?"

"Yes," Ord said.

"Tell that woman to get off her horse and come to me," the man on the chariot said.

"What's going on, Ord?" Vistern asked. "Why did the man on the chariot point at Mud Face?"

"I don't know," Ord said to Vistern.

The man on the chariot rode the chariot nearer to Mud Face. "She's very beautiful," he said. He looked at Ord. "Is she your woman?"

"No," Ord said. He pointed to Vistern. "She's the trader's woman."

"Tell the trader that this woman is coming with me," the man on the chariot said. "The pharaoh will want to see her. He has a fondness for beautiful women."

"Will you tell me what he's saying, Ord?" Vistern asked.

"The man on the chariot wants Mud Face to go with him," Ord said.

"Then tell Mud Face to go with him," Vistern said.

"Mud Face is not going with anyone," Ord said. He looked at Vistern's six guards. "There's going to be a fight," he told them in their language. "I'm not letting him take Mud Face. I'm going to shoot the man on the chariot. When I do, the armed men will shoot at you. Be ready and put an arrow to your bow."

Vistern looked very angry. "You will not shoot him, Ord. Tell him that he can have Mud Face. Tell him."

"What is the trader saying?" the man on the chariot asked.

"The trader's very angry," Ord said. "He will not give you his woman."

The man on the chariot looked angry. "Tell the trader that if he does not give me his woman, I will kill him."

"Why is the man on the chariot looking so angry, Ord?" Vistern asked. "Have you told him that he can have Mud Face?"

"I don't want to go with him, Ord," Mud Face said.

"You will not have to go with him, Mud Face," Ord said. He was pleased to see Vistern's six guards put an arrow to their bows.

"Don't be a fool, Ord," Vistern said. "The ten bowmen will be experts, and you will die if you don't hand over Mud Face."

"If fighting starts, get off your horse and lie on the ground, Mud Face," Ord said.

"There will not be any fighting," Vistern said. "Tell him that he can have Mud Face."

"The trader will not give you his woman," Ord said to the man on the chariot.

The man on the chariot pointed at Vistern and shouted, "kill him."

As several of the Egyptian bowmen shot Vistern, Ord shot the man on the chariot in the chest. Arrows then began to fly in both directions. Ord was relieved to see the six guards shooting at the Egyptian bowmen. From a crouched position on his horse, Ord shot several of the Egyptian bowmen. Ord felt two arrows hit him in the chest.

The shooting stopped. Ord sat up and looked about. All the Egyptian bowmen were lying on the ground. He looked back at Mud Face and Sud, who were lying on the sand, hugging each other. "Are you all right, Mud Face?"

Mud Face sat up. She looked terrified. "Yes. We're all right."

Ord leapt from his horse and cut the throats of the Egyptian bowmen. He then cut the throat of the man who had been riding the chariot.

"Vistern has been shot four times," Haffa said.

Ord walked over to Vistern. He was still alive. "I don't think you're going to live," Ord said.

"Why?" Vistern said. "Why did you do it? You will all die. They will chase you, and you will not get out of the country alive."

"You're a fool, Ord," Haffa said.

Ord ignored her and walked over to two of Vistern's six guards who had been shot. They had both been shot three times and were near to death. "We have to get away from here as fast as we can," Ord told the four guards. "We'll probably be followed by more Egyptians."

"Will we be taking the Egyptian horses with us?" one of the guards asked.

"No. They'll slow us down."

"We should take their horses," the man said. "They're bred for speed and not for endurance like ours."

Ord looked at the Egyptian horses. They did look as if they could run faster than their horses. "What's your name?"

"Fillan," the man said.

"You're right, Fillan," Ord said. "Everyone, change your horses with the Egyptian horses."

Ord walked back to Vistern. He was dead.

"You killed him," Haffa said. "It's your fault he's dead."

"If you don't shut up, I'll leave you here on your own," Ord said to Haffa.

Ord walked over to the man who had been driving the chariot and took off his tunic, his gold necklace, gold rings, gold bracelets, and his animal skin cloak and picked up his huge dagger. He had never seen such a huge dagger. He put his newly acquired possessions into his saddlebag with his other possessions and put them onto one of the Egyptian horses. When they were all mounted on the Egyptian horses, they rode off as fast as they could. He was pleased to see that Sud could ride a horse.

They rode non-stop at a fast pace all day until it was dark, and then continued at a slower pace through the night. Their way was lit by a full moon.

"Why did that man on the chariot want me?" Mud Face asked Ord.

"He wanted to take you to the pharaoh."

"Why?"

"He said that the Pharaoh liked beautiful women."

"If you had not saved me, I would have probably ended up being the pharaoh's woman. I should have hidden my Face. Thanks for protecting me. I only want to be your woman."

"I will always protect you," Ord said.

At dawn, they stopped to let the horses rest and graze for a while. Ord climbed up to a high ridge of ground so that he would be able to see if they were being followed.

Fillan walked up to him. "You're now a very wealthy man, Ord."

"I will be if we can get out of this land without being killed. How is it you know about horses?"

"My father and my brothers breed horses. I was disowned by my father when he found me having sex with a man. Does it shock you?"

Ord was staring into the distance. "No. I already knew that all six of you preferred men to women."

"Doesn't it bother you, Ord?"

"No. Why should it?" Ord turned to look at him and smiled. "As long as you don't want to have sex with me."

Fillan smiled. "There's no chance of that. I already have my partner. We are like you and Mud Face. We would die for each other."

Ord pointed. "Do you see that dust cloud in the distance? I think we're being followed. We need to get going."

They mounted up and continued travelling to the city of stone. From what Ord saw of the men on horseback following them, there looked to be at least fifty. They would not be able to fight fifty armed men and would need to get aboard a boat as quickly as possible. They rode all day and through the night and reached the city at midday. Just before they entered the city, Ord looked back. The men following them were now only a short distance away.

Ord was relieved to see five large boats in the harbour. He dismounted and walked up to a man on one of the boats. "We need to sail to the Minoan island," Ord said.

"When?" the man asked.

"Now."

The man shook his head. "The earliest we can take you is tomorrow."

Ord received the same reply from the men on the other three boats.

Ord was now very worried. He walked up to the man on the last boat. "We need to travel to the Minoan island," Ord said. "We need to go now. We're in a hurry. We have seven horses and seven people. I'll pay you twice what you usually charge."

"That will be four units of gold," the man said.

"I'll give you six units of gold if we can leave straight away," Ord said.

The man stood up and whistled to several men. "Get on board. We're setting sail." He turned to Ord. "Get your horses and the people on board."

While the horses were being put on board the boat, Ord kept looking back to see if the men following them had arrived. He breathed a sigh of relief when the boat began to move out to sea. The men following them arrived in the harbour when the boat had only travelled a distance of about a hundred paces. There were at least a hundred men, and some were riding chariots.

"We only just made it," Mud Face said.

"Yes," Ord said. "It was a good job we changed horses; otherwise, they would have caught us."

"I was very frightened," Sud said.

The man who owned the boat walked up to Ord. He pointed to the men on the harbour. "I gather they were after you?"

"Yes. We only just made it in time. Do you think they will follow us?"

"I don't know. It depends on what you did. What did you do?"

"I killed a priest who was riding a chariot."

The man blew out his cheeks. "That was a very foolish thing to do. You were fortunate to escape. If I were you, I'd get as far away from Egypt as possible."

"I intend to," Ord said. "Will you get into trouble for helping us?"

"No. If the Egyptians did ask me, I'll say that I knew nothing of what you did. You have a strange accent. Where are you from?"

Ord took the world map out of his saddlebag and pointed to his land. "I'm from this island."

"I've never travelled to that land before," the man said.

"Could you take me to that land?" Ord asked.

"No. I don't travel that far. It's a very long way. I could take you part of the way. We'll have to spend the night in the Minoan harbour." He pointed to the map. "I'll then take you to this harbour, and we'll spend the night there. I'll then take you to this harbour, and that's as far as I go. It'll cost you a further six units of gold."

"I'll give you twelve units of gold," Ord said.

Ord sat down next to Mud Face and Sud. He was exhausted. Mud Face and Sud looked frightened. "You're safe now. There's no need to worry."

Mud Face held Ord's arm. "I was so frightened when I saw the men chasing us. I thought they were going to kill us. You were so brave. You could have been killed. You were shot twice. I should have licked your wounds. Do they hurt?"

"No." He had forgotten that he had been shot. He took off his armour and tunic. There were two bruises on his chest and two small cuts. "My armour worked."

She frowned. “Why didn’t the arrows cut into you as much as before when you were shot?”

“Their bows are shorter than normal bows and would not be as powerful as my longbow,” he said. “The short bows are probably easier to use when riding a horse.” He put his tunic and armour back on.

“Thanks for protecting me,” she said.

“You don’t have to thank me. I’ll always protect you.” He pointed to Haffa, who was sitting on her own. “She’s looking very sorry for herself.”

“I don’t care,” Mud Face said. “I don’t like her.”

Fillan sat down next to Ord. “What are your plans for the future, Ord? Do you intend to be a trader?”

“No. I’m thinking of breeding horses. What are your plans?”

“You have a lot of gold, Ord, and we were wondering if you wanted four guards?”

“I would like you to be my guards,” Ord said. “Will you be willing to travel with me to my village?”

“Yes,”

“What will I have to pay you?” Ord asked.

“We’re different to normal men. We have no interest in building huts and having a family. All we require is that we’re provided with food, beer, clothes and a place to sleep. Oh, and a horse.”

“I’ll make sure that you will not want for anything,” Ord said. “What are the names of the others?”

Fillan pointed. “His name is Gorda; he’s Hindern, and he’s Laylan.”

“Tell them that they are now my guards,” Ord said.

Fillan walked to the other men, and Haffa walked up to him. “Thanks for not leaving me in the desert,” she said.

“I should have left you there,” Ord said. “You’re a horrible person.”

“I’m not always a nasty person,” Haffa said. She looked at Mud Face. “I was jealous of you. Not of your looks. I was jealous of your man.” She looked at Ord. “Ord really cares about you. He would even die for you. Most men use women for sex and to look after their children. They don’t care about them.”

“It’s nice to have a man care about you,” Mud Face said. “Didn’t Vistern care about you, Haffa?”

“No. I was just there for sex. He wouldn’t have cared if I had died as long as he had another woman with big breasts to have sex with.”

“Just be nice from now on,” Ord said.

“I will,” Haffa said. “What are you going to do with me?”

"Find you a man," Ord said. He now felt sorry for Haffa. "I'll try and find you a kind man."

"Thank you, Ord," Haffa said.

Chapter Ten

It was getting dark when they sailed into the Minoan harbour. Ord walked over to the man who owned the boat. “What’s your name?” Ord asked.

“Sieed. What’s your name?”

“Ord. If the Egyptians are going to follow us, will they sail the sea at night?”

“No. It’s too dangerous to sail the sea at night, although there is a full moon, so they might set sail and arrive here at dawn.”

“If we did see them at dawn, what could we do?” Ord asked.

“Nothing. If we tried to sail away, they would catch us. They have special boats built for speed that have sails as well as oars. Some of their boats have as many as fifty oarsmen. The good thing in your favour is, I didn’t see any of their fast-sailing boats in the Egyptian harbour.”

They climbed off the boat, lit a fire and ate a meal of cooked fish.

“We would like to have some armour like you, Ord,” Fillan said.

“If you get some stiff hide, Mud Face will make you some armour,” Ord said.

“I will make you some armour,” Mud Face said. “I’m good at making clothes.”

Fillan stood up. “Come on,” he said to the other three guards. “Let’s go and find some stiff hide.”

“The stiffer, the better,” Ord said. “Soft hide is next to useless.”

A short time later, Ord’s four guards returned with some stiff hide.

“Will this hide be good enough, Mud Face?” Fillan asked.

Mud Face examined the hide. “It’s not really stiff enough, but it’ll do.”

Mud Face began making the armour for Ord’s four guards. The others settled down to sleep on the boat, but Ord could not relax. He was worried that the Egyptians would follow them. He stood up and looked out to sea. The full moon would enable him to see an approaching boat, but it would not help him survive. He was on an island and so could not run from them, and there was no way that they would be able to kill a hundred armed Egyptians. They would have to fight and die.

*

As soon as the light of dawn began to filter into their world, they set sail. There was no sign of the Egyptians. Ord tried to convince himself that the Egyptians would not follow them, but he remained unconvinced. Even though the waves were high, this was one time he was glad to be on a boat. Mud Face finished making the armour. She did not look happy.

"Are you all right, Mud Face?" Ord asked.

"No. I feel sick."

"So do I, but I'd rather be sick than fight a hundred Egyptians."

"I feel ill," Sud said. He leaned over the side of the boat and was sick.

Ord and Mud Face smiled at each other.

For something to do, to take his mind off the waves and the Egyptians, Ord showed Mud Face and Sud the gold and gold ornaments he had acquired. "I'm an extremely wealthy man now."

"I've never seen so much gold," she said. "Will you be the leader of the village when we get back? You'll be the richest man in the village."

"No. I won't be the leader, but I'll be a very important man."

Sieed walked over to Ord. "We're being followed, Ord."

Ord was shocked. He stood up. "Where?"

Sieed pointed. "There."

Ord could see the boat in the distance. He began to worry. "Is it an Egyptian boat?"

"I don't know," Sieed said. "It's too far away to tell."

Ord stood looking at the boat. "It's gaining on us, Sieed. Can't we go any faster?"

"No. It has bigger sails than this boat."

"What will happen if it's an Egyptian boat?" Mud Face asked Ord.

"I don't know," Ord said.

"I think it's a Minoan boat," Sieed said. "Yes. It's a Minoan boat. It must have followed us out of the harbour."

Ord breathed a sigh of relief and sat down. "I'll be glad when we get back to our land."

Fillan, Gorda, Hindern and Laylan walked over to Ord.

"There's a boat following us, Ord," Fillan said.

"I know," Ord said. "It's a Minoan boat."

Fillan stood on a box to get a better view and stared at the Minoan boat. "We're being followed by two boats. There's another boat following the Minoan boat."

Ord stood up. "Get off the box and let me see." Fillan climbed off the box. Ord stood on the box and looked at the boats.

"Are we being followed by two boats, Ord?" Sieed asked.

"Yes," Ord said. "No. I think there's another boat in the far distance. I think we're being followed by three boats."

"Let me have a look," Sieed said.

Ord climbed off the box. He began to fear the worst. They were almost certainly being followed by the Egyptians.

Sieed stood on the box and peered into the distance. "We are being followed by three boats. The one nearest to us is a Minoan boat, but I think the other two are the fast-sailing Egyptian boats. They must have sailed through the night from Egypt."

"What are we going to do, Ord?" Fillan asked.

"All we can do is hope that they're not Egyptian boats," Ord said.

"They are Egyptian boats," Sieed said. "They're the fast-sailing Egyptian boats."

"Can we out-sail them and reach land, Sieed?" Ord asked.

"No. We are too far from land, and they're already gaining on us."

They all stood and watched the three boats as they gained on them.

Ord could now see that the Egyptian boats had oarsmen as well as large sails. "How will they attack us, Sieed?"

"I don't know. I hope they will just kill you lot and not me and my men."

"What are we going to do, Ord?" Fillan asked.

"We're going to fight," Ord said. "From what I can see, they have about twenty oarsmen, but I don't think they will do any fighting. They have about forty fighting men on each boat."

"That's eighty-armed fighting men," Fillan said. "I don't think we have eighty arrows."

Ord counted their arrows. They had fifty-three arrows. "We'll have to make every arrow count."

Gorda pointed. "Look. One of the Egyptian boats is pulling alongside the Minoan boat."

They all stood and watched the Egyptian fighting men board the Minoan boat and begin killing the people on board. The Minoans fought back, but they were soon all killed.

"Why are they killing them?" Sieed asked. "They're just sailors and travellers."

"They probably thought that they were us," Ord said.

"They're looking at the horses," Fillan said. "They'll now know that the people on that boat were not the ones they were after, and they'll be coming after us."

Most of the Egyptians climbed back onto their boat, and the rowers began rowing towards them. The other Egyptian boat had caught up, and the two boats began to close in on them. Ord was always optimistic and would fight, but this time he expected to lose and die.

"The Egyptians use large daggers to fight with," Gorda said. "We don't have any large daggers."

Ord took the large dagger out of his saddlebag that he had taken from the Egyptian priest. "They have daggers like these," he said. "When we kill the Egyptians, use their daggers against them."

"I would say that the odds were against us, Ord," Hindern said. "I think we'll need our armour."

"We will," Ord said. "Isn't there anything we can do, Sieed?"

"No, except fight them."

"If we do, we'll probably lose, and you will also die, so try and think of something," Ord said.

"There's nothing we can do," Sieed said. He scratched his chin. "Unless... I wonder."

"What do you wonder?" Ord asked.

"We cannot out-sail them, but we could attempt to sail through The Way of Fools."

Ord frowned. "What do you mean? What is The Way of Fools?"

Sieed pointed. "That is The Way of Fools. We just have time to get there before the Egyptian boats catch us. I don't think the Egyptians will sail through The Way of Fools."

Ord looked to where Sieed was pointing. "I can see the land in the distance, but I can't see anything else."

"The Way of Fools is the only way through the rocks that lie just below the waves at high tide," Sieed said. "It is now high tide, and we cannot see the rocks."

"If we cannot see the rock, how are we going to sail between them?" Ord asked.

"The waves over the rocks are slightly different to the other waves," Sieed said.

"Then sail towards The Way of Fools," Ord said.

Sieed steered the boat towards The Way of Fools. The nearest Egyptian boat was now just behind them.

Ord looked at the waves. They all looked the same to him. "Are we near to the rocks?"

"Yes," Sieed said. "We are now entering The Way of Fools."

"If the Egyptians don't follow us, will we be able to get away?" Ord asked.

"Yes. We'll be able to reach land before they sail around the rocks."

"I think they're following us, Ord," Fillan said.

Ord looked at the Egyptian boats. They were following them. "They'll soon be near enough to board us."

The Egyptians at the front of their boats began firing arrows.

"Take cover," Ord said. "Don't shoot your arrows until they begin to board our boat."

An Egyptian dressed as a priest shouted, "You will all die."

"Yes, but so will you," Ord said under his breath. He intended to make sure that he killed the priest.

They all lay in the bottom of the boat as the two Egyptian boats pulled alongside them; one on each side.

Sieed kept bobbing up and down to make sure they were not sailing towards the rocks. "They'll be boarding us from both sides," he said.

"Be ready to shoot your arrows when they climb onto the boat," Ord said. "When you have used your arrows, use the arrows that have been fired at us."

Mud Face, Haffa and Sud looked terrified.

"Are we going to die, Ord?" Mud Face asked.

"I don't know," Ord said. He pointed. "Hide under them sacks. Because you are women, they might not kill you."

Mud Face and Haffa hid under the sacks.

"What about me?" Sud asked.

"Just hide and hope," Ord said.

The Egyptians began to board the boat from both sides, and while screaming, they shot their arrows. Ord and his bodyguards began to shoot their arrows, and many of the Egyptians were hit.

"There are too many of them," Fillan shouted.

There was a load-crunching sound, and the sails of one of the Egyptian boats lifted high into the air. The men from that boat stopped boarding their boat.

"One of their boats has hit the rocks," Sieed shouted.

They now only had to deal with the Egyptians boarding from one side, but there were still too many of them.

"We're running out of arrows," Hindern shouted.

There was another loud crunching sound, and the sails of the other Egyptian boat lifted high into the air.

"The other boat has hit the rocks," Sieed shouted.

The Egyptians stopped boarding the boat, and Ord and his men only had the ten Egyptian men, who were already on the boat, to deal with. Ord used his last arrow and then attacked the Egyptians using his sword. A short time later, all the Egyptians were dead.

"Cut their throats," Ord said.

When the Egyptians' throats had been cut, Ord looked back at the two Egyptian boats. They were both sinking. "We did it," he said. "We defeated the Egyptians, thanks to you, Sieed."

Sieed looked worried. "We're not safe yet. We could still hit the rocks. This last bit is very difficult to navigate through."

Ord looked at the waves. "They all looked the same to me, Sieed. How can you tell where the rocks are?"

"Experience," Sieed said. He pointed. "That's the last of the rocks there. We've done it. We've sailed through The Way of Fools."

"Well done, Sieed," Ord said. He turned around. "Mud Face. Where are you?"

Mud Face crawled from under the sacks. "I'm here." She stood up and looked at the dozens of dead Egyptians. She looked amazed. "You won. You managed to kill them."

"Yes," Ord said.

Haffa and Sud crawled from under the sacks and stood up.

"I've never been so frightened," Sud said.

Ord and his guards retrieved their arrows, collected the swords that the Egyptians had used and then threw the dead bodies overboard.

"This is one fight I will never forget," Laylan said.

"You've been shot twice, Ord," Mud Face said. "Take off your armour, and I will lick your wounds."

"All of us have been shot," Fillan said. "I hope the armour's worked."

"I've been shot in the leg, but it's only a flesh wound," Laylan said.

Sieed sat watching Ord's men licking each other's wounds and Mud Face licking Ord's wounds, with a frown on his face. "What is this armour you've been wearing, Ord? How does it work?"

"It's just stiff hide that prevents the arrowheads from going into the flesh. It's saved our lives. Are we safe now?"

"I think so," Sieed said. "We should reach the harbour before nightfall."

They pulled into the harbour as the light was fading, ate a meal of fish and slept in a smelly hut. Ord could not believe that they had defeated the Egyptians without any of them getting seriously hurt.

*

At dawn, they set sail again and spent another day being thrown about by the waves. Ord could not relax and expected to see more Egyptian boats following them. As the light began to fade, they pulled into another harbour without seeing any Egyptian boats.

"This is as far as I'm going to take you," Sieed said.

"Thanks for letting us use your boat, and thanks for saving our lives," Ord said as he paid him for the journey.

Sieed smiled. "You and your men were the ones who did the fighting. I just sailed the boat. Your name will always be known as the man who defeated two Egyptian boats in a sea battle. May the gods go with you."

"And may the gods go with you as well, Sieed," Ord said.

They led the horses off the boat.

"We came very close to losing that fight, Ord," Fillan said.

"I know," Ord said.

"I don't think Ord can lose a fight," Laylan said. "He must have the gods with him."

"I think Ord is a god," Hindern said.

Ord smiled. "I don't think so. I'm just a very hungry man. Let's get something to eat."

After eating another meal of fish, they settled down for the night in a hut.

Ord lay down with Mud Face on one side, Sud on the other, Dip at his feet, and the saddlebag containing his possessions under his head. He now had six good friends, seven counting Dip. It felt good to have friends.

"Do you want sex, Ord?" Mud Face asked.

"No. I'm too tired. We can do it tomorrow night."

*

The next day, Ord went to see the leader of the village. Ord was carrying the saddlebag containing his possessions with him. He did not intend to let it out of his sight. He spoke in Vistern's language. "When will we be able to hire a boat?" Ord asked.

"I don't know," the man said. "Our three boats have only just left the harbour. You'll have a wait of at least four days. I can provide you with food and beer and a place to sleep for gold."

"I'll pay you in gold," Ord said.

Ord, Mud Face, Sud and Dip sat on a rock looking out to sea.

"I'm glad you're not going to be a trader, Ord," Mud Face said. "I could never stay on my own, even if I have children, and I hate sailing on the sea. I always feel sick. I hope I never see the sea again."

"You are at this moment looking at the sea, but I know what you mean," Sud said. "I don't like sailing on the sea either."

Ord pointed. “Look at those black clouds. They’re coming this way. We’re in for a storm. Even though it’s not very cold here, it will be in our land.”

“Why?” Mud Face asked.

“It’s winter in our land, and the leaves will have left the trees, and there will be snow on the ground,” Ord said. “Vistern said that it never snows in Egypt. I wonder why?”

“Don’t ask me,” Mud Face said. “I’d rather live in a land with snow than sail the sea.”

It began to rain, and they ran back to the hut, followed by Dip, and sat with Ord’s guards.

Mud Face poked her finger through a hole made by an arrow in Ord’s armour. “You’ll need some new armour,” she said. “If an arrow goes through one of these holes, you will die. If you can get me some stiff hides, I’ll make you some new armour.”

“Could you make us some new armour as well, Mud Face?” Fillan asked. “I think we might need it.”

“Yes,” Mud Face said. “I’ll make you all some new armour. This time, make sure it’s stiff hide. The stiffer, the better.”

*

It took Mud Face two days to make all the armour out of stiff hide. “I’ve made an extra one for you, Ord,” Mud Face said. “I don’t want you getting killed.”

Ord tried the four pieces of armour on. “Four layers of armour are too stiff and too heavy,” he said. “I can hardly move, and I’ll find it difficult to use my bow. I’ll just wear three layers of armour.” He took one of the layers of armour off and walked up and down. “That’s better. Three layers of thick hide will be enough to stop an arrow.”

“I think we might need the armour,” Fillan said. “Look behind you, Ord.”

Ord turned around. Sixteen armed men were riding into the village.

“Tell the men to put on their armour and be ready for trouble,” Ord said.

The riders dismounted, and a huge man, who was wearing several gold rings, began to talk to the leader of the village. The huge man was probably the leader of the tribe. The other men sat down next to the fire.

“You’re not going to fight them, are you, Ord?” Mud Face asked.

“I hope not,” Ord said.

Fillan and the other three guards put on their three layers of armour and stood next to Ord.

"What do you think, Fillan?" Ord asked. "Do they look like trouble to you?"

"Yes, they do. What will we do if they attack us?"

"Fight," Ord said. "The leader is only armed with a large knife. Our problem is the three men with spears. If they attack us, they will spread out and come at us in a line. We must also spread out. I'll kill the men with the spears and the leader."

"We'll shoot the other men," Fillan said.

"Yes, but I don't want you all shooting the same man with the first arrow," Ord said. "The first arrow is very important."

"How will we know which man to shoot?" Fillan asked.

Ord had an idea, so he knelt down and drew in the dirt with his flint knife. "These five marks are us. These sixteen marks are them. You already know not to shoot the leader and the men with spears. I want my man on the left to shoot at the men on the left and my man on the right to shoot at the men on the right. My two men in the middle will shout at the men in the middle, at least with the first couple of arrows. You can then shoot at whoever is still standing. This is the plan we must always use if we have to fight a large number of men."

"It's a brilliant plan," Fillan said. "How did you think of it?"

"I don't know. It's common sense. Just make sure that you're ready for action at all times."

"We will," Fillan said.

"What will me, Sud and Haffa do if fighting starts?" Mud Face asked.

"Hide," Ord said. "Get behind something."

Laylan looked at Ord and shook his head. "You're a very unusual man. You're preparing to fight sixteen dangerous-looking men, and you show no fear. You're very big, but you're only a young man. How old are you?"

"Seventeen," Ord said.

They all looked shocked.

"You're only seventeen?" Fillan said. "I thought you were at least twenty."

The huge man left the leader of the village and, with six of his men, walked over to Ord and his guards.

"Who is the leader of your group?" the huge man asked.

"I am. My name's Ord. Who are you?"

"I'm Durs, the leader of the tribe." He pointed at the horses grazing. "Are those your horses?"

"Yes," Ord said.

"They're fine horses," Durs said. "Do you want to sell them? I'll give you a good price."

"No," Ord said. "They're not for sale."

Durs spread his hands and walked back to the fire with his six men.

"I don't like him?" Mud Face said. "He frightens me."

"He has the arrogance that comes with power," Ord said.

"Do you think he will attack us, Ord?" Fillan asked.

"Yes. I think he just sized us up. He probably thinks that because I'm young, we'll be easy to defeat."

"He's going to be in for a shock if he does attack us," Gorda said. "I just hope they're not very good shots."

"We stand a better chance if they are expert bowmen," Ord said.

Gorda frowned. "Why?"

"Because they will aim for the chest in the same way that the Egyptian bowmen did," Ord said.

"It'll be just my bad luck to have them all shoot their first arrow and the spears at me," Gorda said. "Can the armour stop three spears and sixteen arrows?"

Fillan smiled. "I don't think so."

The day ended without any trouble, and everyone went into the huts for the night.

"It's unlikely that they'll attack us during the night, but I don't want to take the risk," Ord said. "I want someone to keep watch all night. Gorda, you can take the first watch. And don't fall asleep."

Gorda smiled. "I won't."

*

It was a peaceful night. At dawn, Ord left his hut and stretched. The dark clouds had left the sky, and there was not a cloud in sight. He was hoping that the other men would leave today. He had just defecated when the other men began emerging from their huts. The men were looking in his direction, and Ord sensed that something was about to happen.

Ord walked over to his hut. "Come out of the hut. I think they're going to attack us. Haffa, Mud Face and Sud stay inside the hut with Dip."

Ord and his men, with their armour on, walked outside the hut. "What makes you think they intend to attack us?" Fillan asked.

"It was the way the men were looking at me," Ord said.

Durs, followed by his men, walks towards Ord. They looked extremely confident.

"Spread out, put an arrow to your bow and remember what I said," Ord said.

Durs and his men stopped about six paces in front of Ord. They were in a long line and were at a perfect killing distance. "What do you want?" Ord asked.

"I want payment," Durs said.

"What payment?" Ord asked.

"I don't allow people to stop at my village for free," Durs said.

Ord pointed to the leader of the village, who was standing on the other side of the village with his men. "I spoke to the leader of the village, and he didn't say anything about a payment for staying in the village?"

"He's just the leader of the village," Durs said. "I'm the leader of the tribe. I'm a very powerful man. It would take five days to ride from one side of my land to the other. I charge one unit of gold for each person stopping at this village. You owe me seven units of gold."

"If I'd known about the charge to stop here, I would have moved on," Ord said.

Durs shrugged. "It's too late now. You owe me seven units of gold. Are you going to pay me?"

"No," Ord said.

"Then I will have to take your horses," Durs said.

"You will not have my horses," Ord said. "We'll leave your village and stay somewhere else."

"If you don't give me seven units of gold or your horses, I will kill you," Durs said.

Ord decided not to wait until he was shot at, and he shot one of the spearmen in the chest. Arrows began to fly in both directions. Ord shot a second spearman and ducked as a spear flashed past his head. He then shot the third spearman. Durs had moved behind his men, but he was not safe, and Ord shot him in the chest. Ord was shot once in the chest as he killed the last of Durs' men.

Ord took out his flint knife and ran to the prostrate, dying and dead men and cut their throats. He then looked at his men. They all had arrows in their armour. "Is anyone hurt?"

"We've all been shot in the chest," Fillan said. "I think the armour worked."

"I've also been shot in the arm," Hindern said. "It's a glancing wound, and the arrowhead has not gone into the flesh."

They all took off their armour and examined their wounds. The arrows had cut into the flesh, but the arrowheads had not gone into their chests.

"The armour's worked," Laylan said.

Mud Face came out of the hut. "Are you all right, Ord?" she asked.

"Yes. I have a wound for you to lick."

After Mud Face had licked Ord's wound and the men had licked each other's wounds, they put their armour back on.

"This armour is a good idea," Gorda said. "Did you think of it, Ord?"

"Yes. It's heavy to carry around, but it'll save your life. Very few men survive an arrow in the chest."

Ord walked over to the dead men and searched them. Only the leader had anything of value. Ord took his gold rings and the gold he was carrying. "Collect the arrows and see if any of the bows are worth taking," Ord told his men.

The leader of the village walked over to Ord. "I expected Durs to kill you and your men," he said. "He was a greedy man. I had to pay him two units of gold every year."

"Are there any more men like him?" Ord asked.

"No. He was the only dangerous man around here. When they find out that he's dead, they'll elect another leader, and that leader might come after you."

"We'll be gone by then, I hope," Ord said.

Ord walked over to the sixteen horses that had belonged to the men he had killed. The horses now belonged to him. They were not as good as his horses. "I'll sell these horses to you for three units of gold each," Ord said to the leader of the village.

"They're not worth three units of gold each," he said. "I'll give you one unit of gold for each horse."

"They're worth more than that," Ord said. He scratched his chin. "I'll sell you the horses for two units of gold each if you don't charge us for the food and beer we eat while we're here and provide us with provisions for our trip."

The man nodded. "That's a fair price."

The bodies of the dead men were dragged into the forest to be eaten by wild animals, and they sat down by the fire to eat. They had bread and stew. Ord liked stew as long as they cleaned the hot rocks they put into the pot to cook the meat and vegetables.

"I don't know how you managed to kill sixteen men," Sud said.

"It was because they were useless bowmen," Fillan said. "Once they had fired their first arrow, it took them ages to put another arrow to the bow. Most of them only got off one arrow."

"We were very fortunate," Hindern said.

"I think our life with you, Ord, is going to be very exciting," Gorda said.

"Does that bother you?" Ord asked.

Gorda smiled and looked at the other men. "No. We thrive on excitement. I'm already looking forward to the next battle."

Mud Face looked worried. "I hope there's not going to be another battle."

"I think it's inevitable," Fillan said.

*

The bad weather persisted, and they had to wait for another six days for one of the boats to return. It was a large boat and was crewed by five men.

When the owner of the boat was sitting by the fire, eating, Ord walked over to him. "I'd like you to take me to my land," Ord said.

"Where is your land?" the man asked.

"I don't know the name of my land, but I can show you where it is," Ord said. He placed the map of the world in front of the man. "This is my land. I want to go to this part of my land."

"I don't like going that far," he said. "I went there once. It took me seven days to get there and eight days to get back. We call your land The Land of the Savages. Is it a savage land?"

"Not any more savage than the rest of the world," Ord said. "If you did take me there, how much would you charge?"

"I'll not be taking you," the man said. "I'd only take you if I had no work. How many are there in your group?"

"Me, my four guards, two women, a servant and eight horses."

The man blew out his cheeks. "I'd have to charge you eight units of gold, but I wouldn't take you until the spring. The seas are too rough at the moment. When the other boats come in, you could ask them to take you."

"How many days is it to the spring?" Ord asked.

"About sixty days."

"I cannot wait sixty days," Ord said.

Ord walked back to the fire and sat down next to his men, Mud Face, Sud and Haffa. "We'll not be able to sail to my land for sixty days," Ord said.

"It would be quicker to ride," Fillan said. "It'll only take about eight days to reach the sea on the other side of this land. And then it'll only take one day at sea to reach your land."

"I would ride if I knew the way," Ord said. "I don't remember the way we came."

"I know the way," Fillan said. "I've travelled that road many times with Vistern."

"Why didn't you say?" Ord said.

"You didn't ask," Fillan said. "I thought you wanted to sail to your land."

"No," Ord said. "I hate sailing. We'll ride. We'll begin our journey at dawn."

*

After a peaceful night, they set off at dawn. Ord had only sold six of the horses of the men he had killed. He intended to use the others to barter for food and provisions on their journey.

Haffa rode her horse near Ord. "Will you be going to my village?" she asked.

"Is that the village where Vistern was the leader?" Ord asked.

"Yes."

"We will be going to your village," Ord said. "You can stay there if you like."

"I would like to stay there," she said. "I don't want to travel anymore."

"I don't want to travel anymore either," Mud Face said. "Will you be doing any more travelling, Ord?"

"I don't think so. I intend to be a horse breeder. I have eight Egyptian horses to breed from. Six of them are mares, and two are stallions."

Ord rode near to Fillan. "Are we likely to have any trouble on our journey to the sea?" Ord asked. "Do you think we might be attacked?"

"No. We don't stop at the villages where the leaders of the tribes live, and as long as we don't meet any of the leaders on the road, we should not have any trouble."

*

It took them five days to reach Vistern's village. Bruna was still paralysed. Instead of being upset by the news of the death of Vistern, the villagers were overjoyed. The new leader of the village, Tuntern, killed a bullock to celebrate his new appointment.

Ord and his party sat down by the fire and joined in the celebration. The beer made from apples was very tasty and very strong. Ord told Bruna about what had happened to him on his travels. He laughed when Ord told him how Vistern had died.

"I thought you liked Vistern?" Ord said.

"No," Bruna said. "He was the leader of the village and a very powerful man, and I had to pretend to like him. What happened to his gold?"

"I have it," Ord said.

"Then you're a very wealthy man," Bruna said. He looked at Mud Face. "What's so special about Mud Face? What makes you risk your life for her?"

"She keeps me warm at night," Ord said.

Mud Face punched Ord on the arm. "You protect me because you care about me."

"You're a very unusual man, Ord," Bruna said. "Will you now become a trader?"

"No. I like travelling over land, but not across the sea. With the help of my four guards, I intend to breed horses."

Chapter Eleven

It snowed overnight, and the snow was knee-deep by dawn.

In the morning, Sud looked out of the hut. "What has happened, Ord?" he asked. "The world has turned white."

Mud Face pushed past Ord and Sud and walked into the snow. "This white stuff is snow, Sud."

Sud followed her into the snow. "I've never seen anything like it."

Mud Face picked up a handful of snow and threw it at Sud. The two of them then had a snowball fight, with Dip running after the snowballs.

Ord smiled. "I don't know about you two, but I'm getting something to eat."

The three of them walked to the fire and warmed themselves. They were joined by Ord's four guards.

"We'll have to stay here until the snow melts," Ord said.

"I'm freezing," Mud Face said. "I need some winter clothes."

"We all need winter clothes," Fillan said.

"Do you know who would have some winter clothes for sale?" Ord asked a man by the fire.

The man pointed to a tall, thin man. "Bony is the man to see."

Ord bought winter clothes for them all from Bony. After eating their breakfast, they put on their winter fur coats and shoes.

"That's better," Ord said. "I'd forgotten how cold it can get."

It began to snow, and so they all sat under the structure that protected the fire and the people sitting by it from the elements.

"I like snow, but I also hate it," Mud Face said.

"How can you like and hate snow at the same time?" Hindern asked.

"I like the look of snow on the land and trees, but I hate being cold," Mud Face said. "I hate the winters."

Sud pulled his winter fur coat around his body. "I don't like the cold either. Is it always cold in your land?"

"No," Mud Face said. She began to stroke Dip. "We have winters and summers. The winters are cold, but the summers are warm."

"The summers in Egypt are very warm," Sud said. "It gets so hot sometimes you have to find shade, or you will die."

"We'd not be able to wear our armour in Egypt if the summers were that hot," Fillan said.

"Which is one of the reasons why I will never be going back there," Ord said.

"What are the other reasons?" Mud Face asked.

"I don't intend to sail on the sea again when I reach my land," Ord said. "Another reason is I don't want to be chased by hundreds of armed Egyptians."

Haffa came out of her hut and walked up to Ord. "I need your help, Ord," she said.

Ord looked at her. "Why should I help you?"

Haffa sat down next to him. "Because you're a good man. Tuntern, the new leader of the tribe, has selected me to be his woman."

"What's wrong with that?" Ord asked.

"He's a horrible man," Haffa said. "And he's very violent. He already has two wives, and they hate him."

"How can I help?" Ord asked. "If he's already chosen you as his woman, there's nothing I can do."

Haffa pointed to a man standing by a hut. "I want to be that man's woman. He had already chosen me, but he's afraid of Tuntern. I told Tuntern that I'm your woman and that you must decide who has me. Please tell him that you've already given me to that man."

"What should I do, Mud Face?" Ord asked.

"You must help Haffa," Mud Face said. "I don't want her to be with a nasty man."

Ord beckoned the man by the hut over to him. "Did you choose Haffa to be your wife?"

"Yes, but the leader of the village wants her," the man said.

"Do you have a leather bag?" Ord asked.

The man nodded.

"Go and get the bag," Ord said. "That's what I'm charging you for, Haffa. She will then be your woman."

The man hurried off. A short time later, he returned with the leather bag and gave it to Ord. "Thanks for your help," the man said. "What will you do when the leader of the village asks for Haffa?

"I'll tell him that I've already given her to you," Ord said.

"Thank you, Ord," Haffa said, and she walked off with the man.

"Will you fight for Haffa?" Mud Face asked.

"No. I only fight for you."

Sud looked up at Ord. "Will you fight for me?"

"No," Ord said.

"Oh, you must fight for Sud, Ord," Mud Face said. "He's your servant."

"I'll think about it," Ord said.

A short time later, Tuntern walked up to Ord. "Is Haffa your woman?" he asked.

"She was until I sold her to a man in your village for a leather bag," Ord said.

"I would have given you more than a leather bag for Haffa," Tuntern said.

"If I'd known that you wanted her, I would not have sold her," Ord said.

Tuntern walked off.

"What do you think he will do, Ord?" Mud Face asked.

"I don't know, and I don't care."

*

Twelve days later, the snow melted, and Ord and his group set off for the coast.

Ord would be glad to get back to his land where they spoke his native tongue. He had learned a great deal from his travels, but never intended to sail on a boat again, that is, after he had sailed to his land. It was a journey he was not looking forward to.

"What will we be doing when we get back to our village, Ord?" Mud Face asked.

"I intend to breed horses. I'll spend a bit of my gold to buy some animals and some land. I'll also build a new hut for just the two of us. I don't like sharing a hut with my brother and sister."

"I'm looking forward to seeing Helm again," Mud Face said. "And I want the summer to come. I hate the cold weather."

"The winter's almost over now," Ord said.

When they reached the coast, they were greeted by a thunderstorm, and they had to wait for five days for a break in the weather. The sea boat was not as big as the other ones Ord had travelled on previously, and they only just managed to get their party and the horses on board. It was a rough crossing, and they had to bail out continuously. Sud was sick twice. They eventually pulled into a harbour. They had a meal of chicken and bread and spent the night in a hut.

*

At dawn, they had a breakfast of pork and bread. They climbed back onto the boat and sailed along the coast to the harbour where they had departed from with Bruna. It was late in the day when they reached the harbour and led the horses off the boat.

Never again would Ord sail across the moving waters of the sea. “It feels good to be standing on my land,” he said.

Sud looked about. “Is this your land, Ord?” he asked.

“Yes.”

“It looks the same as the land across the sea,” Sud said.

“I know,” Ord said. “Let’s get something to eat.”

They all settled down around a fire and ate fish and bread.

“You will have to learn how to speak my language,” Ord told his four guards.

“We already know some of your words by listening to you talking to Mud Face,” Fillan said.

After they had eaten, they all crowded into a new hut that had just been built. It was very dark inside the hut.

“Do you want sex, Ord?” Mud Face asked.

“Yes. You can go on top.”

“Are you having sex, Ord?” Sud asked.

“Yes, and be quiet, Sud. I don’t like people talking when I have sex.”

Mud Face climbed on top of him. “I’m not getting undressed,” she said. “It’s too cold. Can I talk when we have sex, Ord?”

“Yes. You always do.”

After having sex, he lay down with Mud Face and his saddlebag. It was nice being back in his land and hearing people talking in his mother tongue. He was now eager to get back to his village and tell everyone that he was now a wealthy man.

*

They began their journey at dawn. They travelled at a steady pace, and it took two days to reach his village. The first people they saw when they rode into the village late in the afternoon were Dain and Helm.

“What do you want?” Dain asked.

“It’s Ord,” Helm said, and she threw herself into his arms. “I’m so glad you’re back.” She released him and looked up at him. “I didn’t recognise you at first. I recognised Mud Face. You’ve grown into a man now.”

Dain smiled. “I didn’t recognise you, Ord. I thought you were a trader. You look much older now.”

“Are my animals safe, Dain?” Ord asked.

“Yes. There have been some changes since you left. The tribe up north has taken over our tribe.”

Ord was shocked. “Where’s Serdin?”

“I don’t know,” Dain said. “He left this morning with some of the men.”

Ord saw Old Man sitting by the fire and walked over to him. "What's happened, Old Man?"

"Who are you?" Old Man asked.

"I'm Ord. What's going on?"

"Oh, it's you," Old Man said. "Bad things have happened. About fifty armed men came into the village. They're from the tribe up north. The leader of the tribe, Dromda, said that he was going to be the leader of this tribe as well as his."

"What did Serdin do?" Ord asked.

"What could he do? Dromda had fifty armed men with him. Serdin had to kneel before him."

"I don't suppose it'll be too bad," Ord said. "As long as he doesn't change things."

Old Man spat into the fire. "He already has. He's ordered us to stop building Home of the Gods. We've been told to just have a circle of the healing stones, and the gifts that worshipers pay to touch the healing stones are to be given to Dromda."

"It could be worse," Ord said.

"It is worse," Old Man said. "It's much worse. You came on a horse. I thought you were a trader. Dromda said that traders must not be harmed. Does the horse belong to you?"

"Yes."

"Then you'll have to give it to Dromda," Old Man said. "Only Dromda and his men can have horses. Do you have any gold?"

"Yes."

"Then you'll have to give your gold to Dromda. All gold, silver, copper and tin must be given to Dromda."

"Did Serdin give his gold to Dromda?" Ord asked.

"Yes. Every village must also give animals to Dromda every year: a cow, two sheep or two pigs, depending on the size of the village. Everyone hates Dromda, but they cannot do anything."

Ord walked back to Dain, Helm, his guards, Sud and Mud Face. "We have a problem," Ord said.

"We know," Fillan said. "Dain's just explained what's happened. What are you going to do?"

Ord sat down on a wooden bench outside his hut. "I have three choices. I can accept the new laws, leave or fight."

Fillan smiled. "I know exactly what you will do."

"And what's that?" Ord asked.

"You will fight."

"You cannot fight," Dain said. "Dromda will kill you. He has an army of over a hundred armed men."

Ord picked up a beer jug and took a long drink. It was nice to drink good-quality beer again. He wiped his mouth. "I will fight." He looked at his four guards. "Are you with me?"

"Yes," Fillan said. "What are you going to do? It's going to be very difficult."

"It will be very difficult," Ord said. He stood up and began to pace up and down. "We'll have to plan what we're going to do."

"Serdin will not let you fight," Dain said. "Serdin's decided not to fight. He said it would be foolish."

"Can you now use a bow, Dain?" Ord asked.

"Yes, but even if I fight with you, we'll only have six men against a hundred. It would be extremely foolish to fight them."

"You're right," Ord said. "We'll need more men. I'll have to plan what we're going to do."

Ord walked over to the animal pens and sat on the fence. Dip followed him and sat looking up at him. He needed to be alone so that he could think. Mud Face and Sud walked over to him.

"What are you doing?" she asked.

"I'm trying to think, so be quiet," Ord said. "Go and get me some food."

Mud Face and Sud walked off to get the food.

Ord's thoughts would not work. He could not come up with any ideas on how he could defeat Dromda. Mud Face and Sud returned with some chicken and bread. They gave him the food without speaking and then walked back to Dain, Helm and Ord's guards. Ord ate the food while sitting on the fence. The only idea he could come up with was to try to persuade Serdin to fight Dromda. He climbed off the fence and walked over to the others who were sitting by the fire.

"Have you thought of a plan, Ord?" Hindern asked.

"No. The first thing I'm going to do is to try to persuade Serdin to fight."

"Serdin will not fight," Old Man said. "Serdin's frightened of Dromda."

"Serdin might fight if he can get a hundred men to fight with him," Ord said. He looked about. He could only see old men, women and children. "Does Serdin have all of his armed men with him?"

"Yes," Old Man said. "He's visiting the other villages to see if they will fight."

"Will we be safe here, Ord?" Fillan asked.

Ord chewed his lip. "I don't know. "How often does Dromda visit this village, Old Man?"

"He's been here twice," Old Man said.

Ord had a drink of beer. "There's a possibility that Dromda and his men will visit this village while we're here. If they do, we'll have to make a run for it. The problem we have, is if Dromda is told that men with horses are in this village, he might surround the village with a hundred men. We would then be in very serious trouble."

"What are we going to do?" Laylan asked.

"We cannot risk being trapped," Ord said. "We'll have to camp away from the village." He placed his mouth near to Dain's ear. "We'll be camping by the waterfall," he whispered. "Don't tell anyone where we are. When Serdin returns, come and tell me, and make sure you are not followed."

"I will," Dain said.

Ord purchased food and beer from the villagers to last them for several days and left the village with his guards, Mud Face and Sud. He felt angry and frustrated. He could not understand why Serdin had not put up a fight. It was getting dark when they reached the cave by the waterfall. They lit a fire and sat down outside the small cave.

"What are we going to do if Serdin decides not to fight, Ord?" Fillan asked.

Ord stared at the dancing flames of the fire. "I don't know, any more than I know, why I enjoy looking at flames."

"I enjoy looking at flames as well," Mud Face said. "I also enjoy looking at clouds."

"I enjoy looking at gold," Ord said.

Fillan smiled. "We all like looking at gold."

A short time later, they settled down in the cave for the night.

Ord felt depressed. Maybe tomorrow, he would be able to think of a way to defeat Dromda.

Chapter Twelve

At dawn, Ord walked out of the cave, carrying his saddlebag and sat on a rock by the waterfall. He was filled with frustration. There must be some way to defeat Dromda, but he could not think what it was.

Mud Face sat down next to him. "What are you doing, Ord?" she asked.

"I'm thinking."

"What are you thinking about?"

"I'm trying to think of a plan to defeat Dromda."

She leaned her head against his shoulder. "Do you want me to stop talking so that you can think?"

He sighed. "No. I won't be able to decide what to do until I've spoken to Serdin."

*

At dawn on the third day, after spending two days sitting by the waterfall, Ord saw Dain walking towards him. He stood up. "Are you on your own, Dain?"

"Yes. I've not been followed."

"Why are you here?" Ord asked.

"To tell you that Serdin and his men have returned to the village. They came back last night."

"Good," Ord said. "Get back before you're missed."

Dain ran off.

"What are you going to do, Ord?" Fillan asked.

"Have a word with Serdin and try to persuade him to fight Dromda. I intend to go into the village with you, Fillan, Mud Face and Sud." He pointed to his other three guards. "I want you three to remain outside the village and keep watch for Dromda."

"Will you be fighting Serdin, Ord?" Mud Face asked.

"No. I just want to talk to him."

They climbed onto their horses and rode towards Ord's village.

"If we meet Dromda and his men, do not fight them," Ord said. "Just get away as fast as possible. If we get separated, we'll meet up at the waterfall."

"I like the way you think, Ord," Fillan said. "You have the thoughts of a wise man."

"I just don't want to make any mistakes," Ord said.

Ord, Fillan, Mud Face and Sud rode into Ord's village, and while Mud Face and Sud sat outside Ord's hut and talked to Dain and Helm, Ord and Fillan walked over to Serdin, who was sitting by the fire, eating. Ord did not expect trouble, but he had his bow ready just in case.

"What do you want?" Serdin asked. He sounded angry.

"I want to talk," Ord said.

Serdin took a long drink of beer. "What about?"

"About Dromda."

"Why? Who are you?"

"I'm your son, Ord."

Serdin looked Ord up and down. "I didn't recognise you. I thought you were a trader. I'd been told that you had returned. Why do you want to talk about Dromda?"

"I want to know why you didn't fight him?" Ord asked.

"I wanted to fight, but he had too many men, and he took us by surprise."

"I think we should fight," Ord said. "We could raise an army of our own."

"It would be foolish," Serdin said. "Dromda has an army of over a hundred armed men. And we could not raise an army. I've been to visit most of my villages, but they will not fight. We have no choice but to accept Dromda as our leader."

Ord realised that he was wasting his time talking to Serdin, who was now drunk, and he walked over to his hut. He felt frustrated.

"What are you going to do, Ord?" Fillan asked. "It's obvious that Serdin's not willing to fight?"

"I know. He's too frightened. I don't know what to do. I need to think."

Helm gave Ord a jug of beer. "Do you want something to eat, Ord? I can cook some chicken for you and your men."

Ord sat down outside his hut. "Yes. And can you get us some bread as well?"

"Come with me, Mud Face and Sud," Helm said. "You can help me cook the chickens."

The three of them walked off, and Ord leaned against the wall of his hut. "I'm surprised that Serdin doesn't want to fight. I always thought he was a brave man."

"How many fighting men does Serdin have in the village?" Fillan asked.

"At least fifteen," Ord said.

"If they joined with us, we would still have only twenty-one fighting men," Fillan said. "Twenty-one men cannot defeat a hundred men."

"I know," Ord said. "We need more men."

While Ord ate his food and while the others talked, he tried to decide what to do. It seemed like a hopeless situation.

Dain walked up to Ord. "Are you staying in the village, Ord?" he asked.

"No. We'll be going back to the cave by the waterfall. Don't tell anyone where we are. Don't even tell Helm."

"I won't," Dain said.

Gorda, Hindern and Laylan rode into the village at a gallop.

"Something's wrong," Fillan said.

"Get on your horse, Mud Face and Sud," Ord said as he mounted his horse.

"Armed men are surrounding the village," Laylan shouted. He pointed. "That's the only way out."

The seven of them rode out of the village at a gallop. Three armed men ran from behind some bushes and shot arrows at them, but they all missed, and a short time later, they were well away from the village. They slowed down to a canter.

"You were wise to use us as guards," Hindern said. "Dromda's a wise man, but you are wiser."

"Someone in the village must have informed Dromda's men that we were in the village," Ord said. "We must be very careful."

When they were sitting around a fire outside the cave by the waterfall, Ord tried to decide what to do. "Are you thinking?" Mud Face asked him.

"Yes, be quiet."

By the time he fell asleep in the cave that night, he had decided what he had to do. It was a complicated plan and was full of holes, but it was the only plan he could think of.

*

Just before dawn, Ord walked out of the cave, followed by Dip.

Mud Face ran after him. "Where are you going, Ord?"

"You can come with me if you like."

She held his arm and walked by his side. "What are you going to do? It's still dark."

"I'm going to speak to the sun god."

"I didn't think you believed that the sun was a god?" she said.

"I don't."

They sat down on a log, and he looked towards the east where the sun would rise.

"Why are you going to talk to the sun god if you don't believe the sun is a god?" she asked.

"I want to make sure that the sun is not a god."

She frowned. "What are you going to say to the sun god?"

"I'm going to challenge him."

She stood up. "You're going to challenge the sun god?"

"Yes."

"I'm frightened," she said. "I never know what you're going to do next. I know you don't believe the sun is a god, but I do."

"Why do you believe the sun is a god?" he asked.

"I don't really know. What I don't understand is why everyone believes that the sun is a god if the sun is not a god?"

"Most people are not very clever, and they believe what they're told to believe," he said. "I'm intelligent, and I think deeply about things. I don't believe something just because I'm told to. I want proof that the sun is a god before I believe in him."

"Do you have to challenge the sun god?" she asked.

"Yes. It has to be done."

"Why?" She sat down next to him. "Why do you have to challenge the sun god?"

"I need to know for certain whether the sun is a god or just a light in the sky that provides warmth. Vistern did not believe that the sun is a god. I also believe that the sun is not a god. I don't know what the sun is, but I don't believe it has any power to harm me."

"Then you don't need to challenge him?" she said.

"I do. You still believe that the sun is a god. I need to prove to you, as well as to myself, that the sun is not a god and that it does not have any power."

He climbed upon the log. The sun was about to rise above the horizon. "Do you hear me, sun god?" he shouted.

Mud Face stood up, tripped and fell over the log.

"Do you hear me, sun god?" he shouted. "If you are a god, you will be able to hear me."

Mud Face peered over the log at the horizon where the sun would appear.

"I don't believe you are a god," he said. "You're just the sun. If you are a god, then do not come into our world. Leave us in the dark."

He stood watching the sun rise slowly into his world. "See, Mud Face. The sun is still rising into the sky."

She stood up. "It looks as if the sun is not a god, but I don't like you taking any risks."

"I'm not taking any risks," he said. "Can you hear me, sun god? Mud Face still believes that you are a god. Prove to Mud Face that you are a god. Do something. Do anything."

He waited for a few moments, but nothing happened. "If you are a god, I challenge you to kill me," he shouted. "Can you hear me, sun god? I challenge you to kill me. Go on, kill me."

The sun continued to rise into the sky.

"Are you all right, Ord?" Mud Face asked.

"Yes. If the sun was a god, I would be dead."

Mud Face stood up, climbed onto the log and held his hand.

"What are you doing?" he asked.

"I'm holding your hand."

"Why?"

"I just wanted to. The sun is rising up into the sky as it always does."

"I know," he said. "Vistern was right; the sun does not have any power. It's just an object. Because we don't understand something, it doesn't mean that it is a god. We don't understand how plants grow, but it doesn't mean that plants are gods. Are you now convinced that the sun is not a god?"

"Yes, but why did you have to challenge the sun?"

"I'll tell you when we are all together."

They walked back to the cave, made up the fire and sat down.

She held her hands towards the flames. "I think you are right, Ord. We don't understand what fire is, but it doesn't make fire a god."

"People believe in the gods because they are told to," Ord said. "I want proof before I believe in anything."

Ord's four guards walked up to the fire.

Fillan sat down next to Ord. "I saw you standing on that log, and I heard you shouting. What were you doing?"

"I was planning what to do. I've now decided how I'm going to defeat Dromda."

"How does standing on a log and shouting help you plan?" Laylan asked.

"Vistern did not believe that the sun was a god, and he mocked the sun god, and nothing happened to him," Ord said. "I believe that Vistern was right, but I needed to test whether the sun was powerful or just an object."

"What did you do?" Fillan asked.

"I challenged the sun god to kill me."

The four men, Sud and Mud Face, turned to look at the sun and then turned to face Ord.

"And what happened?" Gorda asked.

"Nothing. The sun did not do anything."

"So, you've proved that the sun is not a god?" Fillan asked.

"Yes. The sun is just an object. The sun does not have any power, and it will always rise into the sky in the morning and sink beyond the hills every evening, despite what we do. Watch." He stood up and raised his hands into the air. "Can you hear me, sun god? You're not a god, and you don't have any power. If you are powerful, then kill me."

The four men, Mud Face and Sud, turned to look at the sun.

Ord waited for a few moments and then sat down. "The sun doesn't have any more power than a tree."

"I agree with you, Ord," Fillan said. "I don't believe that the sun is a god. I don't believe in the gods. I've discussed gods with Vistern, and I agree with him that the only gods are the spirits of our ancestors. What I would like to know is how knowing that the sun is not a god will help us defeat Dromda?"

"That's what I'd like to know as well," Mud Face said.

"I need to raise an army," Ord said. "I need an army if I'm going to defeat Dromda. I need men to accept me as their leader and fight for me."

"I still don't understand how the sun, not being a god, will help you raise an army and defeat Dromda," Laylan said. "I'm getting more and more confused about this."

"I'm going to tell everyone that I'm the new high priest," Ord said.

The men looked at each other and then looked at Ord.

"I don't think they will believe you," Laylan said.

"How are you going to convince them that you're the new high priest when you don't believe in their gods?" Fillan asked.

"I intend to pretend that I believe in their gods. That's why I needed to know whether the gods have any power. Now that I know that the gods are powerless, I can forget about upsetting them.

"I'm still confused," Laylan said.

Ord smiled. "You will eventually understand, Laylan. The people will follow me and do what I want if they think that the gods are on my side."

"Oh," Laylan said. "So, if you convince people that you're a high priest, you expect them to do what you want?"

"Yes," Ord said.

"It's going to be very difficult to convince people that you're a high priest," Gorda said. "How are you going to do it?"

"It is going to be very difficult," Ord said. "I intend to dress up as a high priest and return to my village and kill Serdin. I'll tell the villagers that the gods have spoken to me and that the gods want us to fight Dromda and kill him."

"When are we going?" Hindern asked.

"As soon as I've changed into a high priest," Ord said.

"How are you going to change into a high priest?" Mud face asked.

"Just watch," Ord said.

They all stood and watched Ord put the white tunic over his armour, put the large gold necklace around his neck, put the leopard skin over his shoulders, and pull the sword out of its scabbard.

"What do you think?" Ord asked. "Will I convince them that I'm a high priest?"

"I think you will," Fillan said. "Your plan is brilliant."

"You look like a very important man," Sud said.

Mud Face walked around Ord, looking him up and down. "I think you will convince them that you are a high priest."

"Then let's see if it works," Ord said. "When we ride into the village, Mud Face and Sud, I want you to go and stand with Dain and Helm. I don't want you getting hurt. I'll approach Serdin with my guards and tell him that I'm going to be the leader of the tribe and that I'm going to fight Dromda. He'll not accept me as his leader, and so I intend to kill him with the sword." He turned to face his four guards. "I want you to be ready to kill any man who puts an arrow to his bow."

"We will be ready," Fillan said.

They climbed onto their horses and rode towards the village.

"I think your plan will work," Laylan said.

"I hope so," Ord said. "It's the only plan I can think of, and we have to do something sooner rather than later. Someone's bound to discover that we're camped by the waterfall, and Dromda will eventually be told, and he might bring an army against us before we are ready to fight him."

"Vistern was right," Gorda said. "He said that you would one day be a leader of men."

"I hope Vistern was right and that this will be the day," Ord said.

Everyone in the village stopped and stared at them as they rode into the village.

Ord smiled. Even though what he was doing was dangerous, he was confident that his plan would work. Serdin, who was sitting by the fire surrounded by his men, stood up when he saw Ord. Ord, who had his bow and arrows and his sword with him, climbed off his horse and walked up to Serdin.

Ord's four bodyguards also climbed off their horses and followed him. Mud Face and Sud climbed off their horses and stood next to Dain and Helm.

"Why are you dressed like that?" Serdin asked.

Ord stopped in front of Serdin. Ord was now within striking distance of Serdin. "I've come to tell you that we will be fighting Dromda."

"We will not be fighting Dromda," Serdin said. "We do not have the men to fight."

"We do," Ord said. "But you're not strong enough to lead them."

"What?" Serdin shouted. "Get out of my village, or I will kill you."

"I am now the leader of this tribe," Ord said. "And I give the orders."

"No, you're not," Serdin shouted, and he lunged at Ord.

Ord pulled the sword out of its scabbard and slashed Serdin's throat. Serdin fell to the ground.

No one moved except Ord's brother, Leenon, who put an arrow to his bow. Fillan shot him in the chest, and he fell to the ground.

While Serdin was clutching his throat and dying, Ord turned to face the people of the village. "Get on your knees," Ord shouted.

Everyone, even Ord's four guards, knelt down on one knee. To kneel on one knee signified that they would follow Ord, even into battle.

"Stand up," Ord Shouted.

The villagers stood up and looked about nervously.

"I am now the leader of this tribe, and I will now tell you what we're going to do," Ord said. "I am invincible. The gods have spoken to me. I have been chosen by the gods to be the high priest of the gods. The wind is the voice of the gods, and it has told me what to do."

The wind suddenly began to blow strongly, and while still holding his sword, he raised his hands into the air and faced the wind. "I hear your words," Ord shouted as the wind blew through his hair. "We're ready to fight, and we'll make sure that Home of the Gods will be built. We will not let you down." He was pleased to see fear on the faces of the men.

The wind stopped blowing, and Ord put his hands down. "The gods have told us to fight, Dromda. We will fight. We will fight." The men joined in, and they all began shouting, "We will fight."

When the shouting eventually stopped, Ord sat down by the fire. The villagers were looking at him as if he were a god. "Bring me some food and some beer," he told one of the men.

"Yes, Ord," the man said, and he hurried off.

"The gods are with us," one of the men said.

Fillan sat down next to Ord. "You never fail to amaze me. You now have every man here willing to die for you."

Ord smiled. "The first part of my plan has worked. We'll execute the second part of my plan tomorrow."

"And what's that?" Fillan asked.

"To tell the rest of the tribe that I'm now their leader and that we're going to fight Dromda."

It was almost dark when Ord had finished eating. He felt exhausted. He stood up and pointed to four men. "I want you four men to stand guard just outside the village all night. One to the north, one to the south, one to the west and one to the east. If you see anyone approaching the village, let me know immediately."

"We will, Ord," one of the men said.

Ord took the saddlebag off his horse, containing his possessions, and pointed. "That was Vistern's hut, Fillan. It's now your hut to share with Gorda, Hindern and Laylan. I'm going to my hut."

Ord walked towards his hut, followed by Dip, Mud Face and Sud.

"Even though I told Dain that you could not be killed, I was very frightened," Mud Face said.

"You should not have worried, Mud Face," Ord said. "I'm invincible." He stopped and stared at Sud. "What are you doing?"

"Nothing," Sud said.

"Where are you going?" Ord asked Sud.

"With you and Mud Face to sleep in your hut."

Ord pointed. "You can go and sleep with my guards in their hut," Ord said.

"Why?" Sud asked. "Why can't I sleep with you and Mud Face?"

"Go on, Ord," Mud Face said. "Let Sud sleep with us. He's your servant, and you'll need your servant to be near you. There's plenty of room in our hut with Dain and Helm."

"Okay," Ord said. He looked up.

"What are you looking at?" Mud Face asked.

"The moon," Ord said. "It's very bright tonight. I know your secret moon. I know you're not a god and that you have no power. If you are a god, then do something." He was speaking quietly so that the villagers would not hear what he was saying.

For a while, Ord, Mud Face and Sud stood looking up at the moon and stars and the clouds moving across the sky.

"The moon is not a god," Ord said. "It's just an object like clouds. I wonder how far the moon is away from us."

"It doesn't make any difference how far it is away from us; we cannot touch it," Mud Face said.

"What do you think the moon is made of, Ord?" Sud asked.

"I don't know," Ord said. He pointed. "That star doesn't move. The other stars move around that star. We call it the North Star. By looking at that star, we can tell which way is north at night."

"Why would you want to know which way was north at night?" Mud Face asked.

"I don't know," Ord said. "Let's go to sleep. I've had a very tiring day, and I've got a big day ahead of me tomorrow."

Chapter Thirteen

Ord was woken up by Mud Face playing with Dip and tickling his stomach. "Who's a good dog?" she said.

He smiled. "You look happy, Mud Face."

"I am happy."

"Why?" he asked. "We have many dangerous things to do yet."

She pulled back the hide that covered the entrance to their hut and pointed. "That's the reason why I'm happy."

He pulled on his armour, picked up his bow and arrows, stepped out of the hut and looked about. It was dawn, and the light of a new day was creeping into his world. "I can't see anything to be happy about."

"The reason for my happiness has not arrived yet," she said.

He frowned. "Not yet arrived. When will the reason for your happiness arrive?"

She smiled. "It's beginning to arrive now."

He looked about. His horses were beginning to graze, and people were emerging from their huts. "Is this reason for your happiness a person?"

"No." She began to laugh. "I thought you would have guessed by now."

When she laughed, she was even more beautiful. "You're a very beautiful woman."

"Am I really beautiful?" she asked.

"Yes. You're the most beautiful woman in the world."

"Are you saying that just to make me happy?" she asked.

"No. I mean every word of what I say."

"I wish I could see my face like you see it," she said. "When I look in water, the reflection's not very clear." She looked up at him. "Do you realise how handsome you are?"

"I'm the same as you. I cannot see what I look like." He then had an idea. "I think there is a way to see what we look like."

"Where are you going?" she asked.

"I'm going into the hut."

"Why?"

"To get a reflector."

She put her hands on her hips. "And what's a reflector?"

He took a silver plate out of his possessions. "This is what some wealthy Minoans and Egyptians eat off."

"What is?" she asked.

"This." He polished the flat part of the silver plate with his tunic and looked at his reflection. A very handsome, mature and very confident-looking man stared back at him. "I didn't realise I looked like that," he said.

"Does it reflect your image?" she asked.

"Yes."

"Let me look at my image," she said.

He handed her the plate.

She stared at her image without speaking.

"What's wrong?" he asked.

She looked at him and then looked back at her image.

"Can you see what you look like?" he asked.

"I don't know."

He frowned. "Isn't it working?"

"I don't know," she said. "The reflection is of a very beautiful woman. I don't think it's my reflection."

He looked over her shoulder at the reflection. "It is your reflection. You are a very beautiful woman."

"I feel strange," she said. "I didn't realise I was so beautiful. It's no wonder men wanted me as their woman."

He looked about. "I still can't see the reason for your happiness. Has it arrived yet?"

"Yes."

"Where is it?"

She pointed. "It's there."

He looked to where she was pointing. "Where? All I can see are clouds."

"It's hiding behind the clouds." She hugged him. "I'm glad I'm beautiful. Does it make you happy to have a beautiful wife?"

"It makes me very happy to have a beautiful wife, although she can be very frustrating at times. What can be hiding behind clouds?"

She smiled up at him. "You now know how handsome you are. There can only be one thing hiding behind the clouds. What is it?"

"It's the sun," he said. "Why does the sun make you happy?"

"I'm happy because you are right," she said. "The sun is not a god, and it does not have any power; otherwise, you would be dead, or the sun would not have risen into the heavens. I'm happy because I now know that the sun is just an object."

He smiled. "I'm glad you're happy; just don't tell anyone that we don't believe in the gods. They will not understand."

"I won't, but we do believe in the spirits of our ancestors, don't we?"

"Yes, although I don't believe we should sacrifice to the dead spirits. I don't believe they can help us or harm us. It just helps to believe that we go to a nice place when we die."

"It does," she said. "I like to think that we'll go to a nice place when we die."

"What happens in life depends on what we do," he said. "If we make mistakes, we suffer, and if we make the right decisions, we prosper. And it doesn't matter what sacrifices we make to the gods. We will all suffer from some ailments and will eventually get old and die."

He walked back into his hut.

She followed him. "What are you doing?" she asked.

"I'm going to dress as a priest." He put on his tunic and his gold necklace and put the leopard-skin cloak over his shoulders. "I'll need to convince the rest of the tribe that I'm a holy man. Let's get some food to eat."

Ord and Mud Face sat down by the fire, ate breakfast and drank a jug of beer. He was very proud of what he had achieved. He was now regarded as the leader of the tribe and as the high priest by his village. What he had to do now, before he could attack Dromda, was to convince the rest of the tribe that he was a high priest and get their allegiance. And even though he did not believe in their five gods, he intended to pretend that he did and use the fear of the gods that his people had to control them.

"Everyone's staring at you," Mud Face whispered.

He smiled. "I know."

Fillan sat down next to Ord. "You look very impressive, Ord," he said. "Why are you dressed like that?"

"I intend to dress like this every day. I need to convince the other villagers that I'm a high priest."

"We've been talking to the villagers and telling them about what a great fighter you are, Ord," Fillan said. "We told them how you defeated the Egyptians and several tribe leaders."

"Did you exaggerate what I did?" Ord asked.

Fillan smiled. "Yes, little."

"Good," Ord said.

"We've been talking to Morteen," Fillan said. "He thinks you intend to kill him."

"Dain," Ord said. "Go and tell Morteen to come here."

Dain ran off and returned with Morteen.

"Sit down, Morteen," Ord said.

Morteen sat down. “I accept you as the leader, Ord. There’s no need to kill me. I’ll do exactly what you want.”

“I don’t intend to kill you, Morteen.” The villagers were listening, and so Ord had to be careful about what he said. “I don’t intend to kill anyone as long as they do what I say. I’ve spoken to the gods. The wind has told me to be the high priest of all this land and to start building the Home of the Gods. You, Morteen, and Old Man and the other wise men, will assist me. But first, I’ll be visiting all the villages in my tribe to tell them what my plans are and raise an army to defeat Dromda.”

Morteen looked relieved. “The men are ready to fight for you. Now that you are the high priest, what will my job be?”

“I’ll be the high priest of all this land, but you will still be the holy man, and you will continue to do what you’ve always done. I’ll still need holy men to offer the sacrifices to the gods at the many festivals we have.”

“I didn’t want them to stop building the Home of the Gods,” Morteen said. “It was Dromda’s idea. What are you going to do with Dromda?”

“Kill him, but first, I need to visit all the villages in my tribe and tell them that we’ll be fighting Dromda. Go and tell all the fighting men to get ready to leave.”

“Yes, Ord,” Morteen said, and he hurried off.

“I’m leaving in a short time with my men and Mud Face, Sud,” Ord said. “I want you to stay in the village. You can help Helm feed the animals.”

Sud nodded.

A short time later, all the fighting men were assembled in the village.

“There are only twelve fighting men,” Fillan said. “With us, that’s a total of seventeen fighting men. How can we defeat Dromda with only seventeen men?”

“We cannot,” Ord said. “That’s why we need more men from the other villages.”

Ord left the village with provisions to last for five days and with all the men who were able to fight. The men were armed and followed Ord, Mud Face and his four guards, who were riding their horses.

Mud Face looked worried. “What’s wrong, Mud Face?” Ord asked.

“Why am I going with you?” she asked. “I’m just a woman.”

He smiled. “I don’t expect you to fight. I’m taking my gold and my precious possessions with me because I don’t want them stolen. You are my most precious possession. I’m taking you with me so that I can protect you. I don’t want you harmed.”

"How are we going to defeat Dromda?" Fillan asked. "They say he has an army of five hundred men."

"I've been thinking about that. I'm hoping he doesn't have as many as five hundred men. I intend to kill him as soon as possible before he realises that we've decided to fight him. I intend to get all the fighting men from my tribe to fight with us."

"If you do get all the fighting men in your tribe to fight with you, how many fighting men will we have?" Fillan asked.

"Our tribe is not as big as Dromda's tribe. There are only fifteen villages in our tribe, and some of them are very small. We should be able to raise about a hundred fighting men."

"How are we going to defeat five hundred men with one hundred men?" Fillan asked.

"I've also given that some thought. If we give Dromda time to raise his army of five hundred men, we'll be defeated. Dromda lives in a very large village that contains at least thirty and as many as fifty fighting men. When we've gathered all our fighting men together, we'll attack Dromda's village at dawn. Even though their dogs will bark and warn them, we should be able to shoot them as they come out of their huts. The entrances to all huts always face towards the rising sun, so we'll attack from the west. You and my other bodyguards will stay close to me. Our job will be to kill Dromda as he comes out of his hut."

"The plan is dangerous, but it's a good plan, and it should work," Fillan said.

"If we can kill Dromda, we should not have any problems with the rest of his tribe," Ord said. "They'll stop fighting when their leader is dead."

"Will you stop at being the leader of two tribes, or will you take over more tribes?" Fillan asked.

Ord thought for a few moments. "I don't know. If I do, it'll be to take over the tribes to our west, east and south."

Ord rode into the nearest village to his village. "Stay at the back of the men, Mud Face," he said. He then realised his mistake, turned around and galloped out of the village. His men and Mud Face followed him. They were not followed, so they slowed down so that the men who were walking could catch up.

"What's wrong?" Fillan asked. "Why have we run away?"

Ord was angry with himself. "I nearly made a big mistake. The village we were just in is the largest of the villages in the tribe and has at least twenty fighting men."

"What difference would that make?" Fillan asked. "I thought we wanted fighting men?"

"We do. The leader of that village is a strong-willed man, and he might not accept me as his leader. If we had to fight him, we could lose most of our men. We could even have been defeated."

"You made a wise decision, Ord," Fillan said. "I gather we'll now be visiting a small village?"

"Yes. We'll visit the smallest villages first and work our way up to the largest."

The smallest village only contained six huts. Ord told Mud Face to stay back and rode into the village with his men. "This village only has seven fighting men," Ord said. "The leader of this village is a man named Thunder."

Ord stopped in front of Thunder and climbed off his horse. Ord's four bodyguards also climbed off their horses.

"I've told Dromda that we don't have any more gold," Thunder said.

"I'm not one of Dromda's men," Ord said. "I'm Ord. I'm the new high priest of all the land. I'm also the new leader of your tribe. Dromda is no longer your leader; I am."

Thunder looked confused. "I don't understand. Have you killed Dromda?"

"No," Ord said. "But I intend to. I'm raising an army to fight him." Ord raised his sword and his bow into the air. "I'm the leader of this tribe. Death to Dromda. Death to Dromda."

His men joined in and began to shout, "Death to Dromda. Death to Dromda."

It was obvious to Ord that Thunder had been intimidated and was now too frightened to fight him. Ord silenced his men. "Get on your knees before me," Ord shouted. Thunder, his men, the villagers and Ord's men sank onto one knee.

"I have spoken to the gods," Ord said. "The gods have told me to raise an army and to kill Dromda, and start to build the Home of the Gods. Stand up."

Everyone stood up.

"You're now my people," Ord said. "I'm your leader. Everything will now return to how it used to be. From now on, you'll be able to own gold and other precious metals and horses."

"Will the fighting men of this village be going with you, Ord?" Thunder asked.

"Yes. Tell all your fighting men to gather provisions to last for about four days and follow me."

A short time later, Ord and his small army of twenty-eight fighting men left the village.

"It's a pleasure to see you in action, Ord," Fillan said. "You were born to be a leader of men."

"I'm slowly getting the hang of it," Ord said.

Over the next two days, Ord and his men visited all but one of the villages in his tribe and recruited all their fighting men. There was now just one village to visit. It was the largest of the villages that he had entered by mistake. Ord told Mud Face to wait outside the village, and he rode into the village with his men. He stopped his horse in front of the leader of the village, whose name was Hind.

"Who are you, and what do you want?" Hind asked. He was a big, aggressive man and was known for having a vicious temper.

"I'm the new leader of the tribe," Ord said.

"Serdin's the leader of our tribe?" Hind said.

"He's no longer the leader of the tribe." Ord had a feeling that he would have to kill this very arrogant man. Hind was surrounded by twenty armed men who already had an arrow to their bow. Ord now had nearly a hundred fighting men with him, and he was confident that he would win if a fight started. "I killed Serdin, and I'll kill any man who does not kneel before me. Get on your knees."

Hind and his fighting men did not kneel on one knee. Ord sensed that there could be a fight.

"Even if you are the leader of this tribe, you will have to answer to Dromda," Hind said. "I only answer to Dromda."

Ord climbed off his horse. His patience had run out. "Are you going to kneel before me, Hind?"

"No," Hind said. "Dromda will kill me if I do."

Ord shot Hind in the throat, and he fell to the ground. One of Hind's men aimed his bow at Ord and was shot. Three arrows hit his chest, and he fell to the ground before he could shoot his arrow.

"Get on your knees," Ord shouted to Hind's fighting men.

Without hesitating, all of Hind's fighting men, the villagers and Ord's fighting men sank onto one knee.

For a while, Ord stood in front of his people. Being a leader gave him immense power, and he intended to use it wisely. "Stand up."

Everyone stood up.

"All the fighting men in this village are to get food and possessions to last for a few days and follow me," Ord said. "We're going to fight Dromda." He raised his bow and his sword high in the air and shouted, "I am invincible."

All the men began shouting, "Ord is invincible. Ord is invincible."

After a short time, Ord silenced them and pointed to one of the men. "Bring me some food and beer."

Ord sat down by the fire with Mud Face and his bodyguards and ate a meal of rabbit, bread and beer.

"I watched you shoot your arrow, Ord," Mud Face said. "You can shoot an arrow much faster than the other men. How do you do it?"

His men were listening, and he had to be careful what he said. "I was taught by the gods. They also taught me to speak the languages of other lands. I have the gods with me, which is why I'm invincible."

Mud Face smiled. "Will I be going with you when you go to fight with Dromda?"

"Yes. I cannot afford to leave any of my men behind to protect you. Just make sure you stand out of the reach of the arrows when the fighting starts."

"I will," she said. "What will you do when you are the leader of both tribes?"

Ord chewed his lip. "I don't know. I've never been the leader of two tribes before. I'll ask the gods. They will tell me what to do. I suppose I'll sort out any disputes and organise the festivals and the building of the Home of the Gods."

"Do you still intend to breed horses, Ord?" Fillan asked.

"Yes. These Egyptian horses are much better than other horses. If we breed from them, we'll become very wealthy."

After they had finished their meal, Ord led his army of over a hundred men and headed for his village. He was now in a position to defeat Dromda. It was late in the day when he reached his village. He ordered four men to stand guard outside the village and sat down by the fire to eat and drink. It had been a tiring day, and he was already falling asleep. After eating, he stood up. "Let's go into our hut to sleep, Mud Face."

They entered his hut.

He took off his cloak, tunic, and armour and lay down on his bed. "I'd much rather sleep in my bed than out in the open," he said.

"I do as well," Mud Face said. "Do you want to have sex?"

"Yes. You can go on top."

She climbed on top of him and sank down onto his erect penis. After they had had sex, they lay down together. He was very pleased with his life. And even though tomorrow he would be fighting Dromda, he was not fazed in the slightest. His confidence was so high, he felt that he had already won.

Chapter Fourteen

At dawn, after eating breakfast, Ord, his men and Mud Face set off and headed towards Dromda's village. This time Ord was not wearing his gold necklace, white tunic and the leopard-skin cloak. They would get in the way when the fighting started. They travelled at a brisk pace, and even though they kept clear of the villages, they still met four men and two women. "Make sure that they stay with us until we reach Dromda's village," Ord told his men.

Mud Face looked back at the four men and two women who were being led along. "Why are we taking them with us, Ord?"

"They are people from Dromda's tribe, and they might tell Dromda that an army of men is approaching his village. He would then be waiting for us with his army of five hundred men. To win, I need to surprise Dromda."

They did not meet any more travellers and settled down for the night by a stream. Ord lay down under a tree with Mud Face, Dip and his saddlebag. For his plan to work, he would have to surprise Dromda. If Dromda had been told about Ord and his men, Dromda would probably ambush him, and it could be disastrous.

*

At dawn, Ord and Mud Face had breakfast of chicken, bread, and beer, which they had brought with them, and then continued their journey.

"Send some men on ahead to look for other travellers and for Dromda's men," Ord told Fillan.

They met four other travellers on their journey and took them along with them. When they were a short distance from Dromda's, village, they stopped. It was beginning to get dark.

"What do we do now, Ord?" Fillan asked.

"Tell the men to hide as best they can and be quiet, and tell them not to light fires. Tell them that we'll be attacking Dromda's village at the first light of dawn."

Ord sat under a tree with Mud Face and Dip. He was tired, but found it difficult to sleep. His mind was full of worries about what could go wrong with his fight with Dromda. Ord was hoping that Dromda had fifty or fewer fighting men with him in the village. If Dromda had five hundred fighting men with him and Ord was unable to kill Dromda, all would be lost.

Mud Face fell asleep, and Ord sat looking up at the stars. His world was full of things he did not understand. Stars looked like sparks from a fire. Even though Egyptian pharaohs believed that they became stars when they died, he believed that stars were not alive. They were just objects. The moon appeared and began to move slowly across the sky. The moon looked like a light underneath a thin animal skin. A few clouds appeared. Clouds were probably the breath of the wind. If only he had a greater understanding of his world.

*

Someone was shaking Ord's arm. It was Fillan. Ord sat up. "Is something wrong?"

"No. You asked me to wake you up before dawn. It will soon be getting light."

Ord stood up and stretched. "Get the men ready."

"They are ready. We're just waiting for you to lead us to victory."

Mud Face stood up. "What do you want me to do?"

"I want you to keep well away from the fighting and look after my bag of gold," Ord said. "I don't want you getting hurt."

As Ord and his men moved silently towards Dromda's village, Ord began to worry about Mud Face. He called two men over to him. "I want you to stay with Mud Face and guard her with your life. If anything happens to her, you will die."

"We will protect her, Ord," one of the men said.

"I've just spoken to a man who's been to Dromda's village," Fillan said. "He said that we are now only a short distance from the village, and the dogs will soon begin to bark."

"Tell the men to run towards the village when the dogs begin to bark and shoot the men as they come out of their huts," Ord said. "We'll be riding our horses, and we'll be able to get into the village first and should be able to kill Dromda when he comes out of his hut. I've been told that he lives in the biggest hut in the village. Get behind the men now, Mud Face. I'll see you when I've killed Dromda."

"The thing I admire the most about you, Ord, is that you have no fear," Fillan said.

"Fear is a waste of an emotion," Ord said.

When the village huts came into view, the dogs began to bark, and Ord and his bodyguards began to gallop into the village, followed by his men, who were running. An arrow hit Ord in the chest, but he did not shoot back. His aim was to kill Dromda.

The barking of dogs and the screaming of men and women filled the air as the arrows began to fly. As Ord pulled up outside the largest hut in the village, Dromda ran out, and Ord shot him in the chest. While sitting on their horses,

Ord and his guards began shooting Dromda's men. A short time later, Dromda's men realised that their leader was dead, and threw their bows to the ground. The fight was over.

Ord climbed off his horse and examined Dromda. He was dead. Ord slit his throat and then slit the throats of the five Dromda men who had been shot and who we either dead or dying. He then checked on his men. Four had been shot and would probably die. Ord pulled two arrows out of his armour. Gorda and Hindern had also been shot.

"Let's see if our armour's worked," Ord said.

Ord, Gorda and Hindern took off their armour and examined their wounds. The flint arrowheads had left just small cuts in the skin. While the bodyguards licked each other's wounds, Mud Face licked his wounds.

"We did it, Mud Face," Ord said. "We killed Dromda. I'm now the leader of two tribes."

She looked up at him and smiled. "I think you are invincible."

Ord watched his men collecting their arrows. "I didn't realise that the men were such bad shots. It was a wonder that anyone was shot. We were fortunate that Dromda's men were also bad shots. You, Fillan, are a good shot, and so are you, Laylan, but you, Gorda and Hindern need to practice."

"We will," Gorda said. "I didn't hit one man."

Ord's men and the whole tribe were now gathered around him. He climbed onto a large log. "I am now the leader of your tribe. Get on your knees."

The whole tribe and his men knelt on one knee.

Ord smiled. He was surrounded by over a hundred and fifty men. "You can now stand up."

The men stood up and began to shout, "Ord is invincible. Ord is invincible."

Ord waited for a while, listening to the praise of his men and then jumped off the log. "Bring me something to eat and drink," he told a man.

"Yes, Ord," the man said, and he hurried off.

Ord sat down by the fire and was given meat and beer. He took a long drink and began to eat the meat.

An old man walked towards him. He knelt on one knee. "I'm not a fighting man," he said. "I hid with the wise men and the old men when the fighting started."

"Who are you?" Ord asked.

"I'm the holy man. I've been told that you're now the holy man. Will you be killing me?"

"No. You are still the holy man. I am the high priest. All the holy men answer to me. I'm the high priest of all the land. I've been told by the gods to build the Home of the Gods. You can help us build the Home of the Gods."

The man looked relieved. "I will help you, Ord."

"I need to appoint a leader of this village," Ord said. "Who do you think should be the leader?"

"Winch should be the leader of this village," the holy man said. "He's a good man."

"Go and tell Winch and the wise men that I want to speak to them," Ord said.

"Yes, Ord," the holy man said, and he hurried off.

A short time later, a tall young man and six old men walked towards him.

"Are you Winch?" Ord asked the tall young man.

The tall man nodded. He looked frightened.

"I need a man to be the leader of this village," Ord said to Winch. "Do you want the job?"

"Yes, Ord," Winch said.

"Then you have the job, Winch," Ord said. He looked at the old men. "Which one of you is the wisest?"

Five of the old men looked at the same man. "What's your name?" Ord asked the man they were looking at."

"Randin," the old man said.

"I'll need wise men to help me build the Home of the Gods, so you will be coming with me to my village," Ord said.

"Will we have to give you our gold and silver, Ord?" Winch asked.

"No," Ord said. "Tell the villages that the men can keep their gold and silver, and if they can afford a horse, they can have one. Every village will be required to make a payment to me each year. What they give me will depend on the size and wealth of the village. I'll decide on how much later on. I will also need one man from each village to help in the building of the Home of the Gods."

"I'll send the men to your village, Ord," Winch said.

After eating, Ord and his party began the return journey to his village. He felt very pleased with himself and was looking forward to breeding horses and building the Home of the Gods.

"I watched the fight," Mud Face said. "I saw you kill Dromda. You're so accurate with your arrows."

"It's thanks…" Ord had almost said that it was thanks to all the practice he had when he had been minding the animals. Many of the men were in earshot and would hear what he was saying. He winked at Mud Face. “It’s thanks to the gods. The gods make sure that I never miss.”

Mud Face realised he was lying and smiled.

Chapter Fifteen

Ord walked out of his hut. It was dawn. He was wearing his gold necklace and his leopard-skin robe and was carrying his sword. He had been the leader of both tribes for six days. Twenty-five men had been assembled and were ready to begin moving the large god stones to the Home of the Gods. The cart had been loaded up with rope, tools and provisions. Ord sat down by the fire with Morteen, Randin, Old Man and several other wise men.

"The large stones for building the five temples to the gods have already been prepared," Ord said. "Randin and Morteen, I want you to organise the men and start bringing the stones to the Home of the Gods. While this is being done, get the holes dug in the correct places where the god stones are to be erected."

"The holes have already been dug, Ord," Morteen said. "The healing stones have been moved, and the men are building the earth ramps."

"Good," Ord said. "I intend to travel to the Home of the Gods today."

Randin, Morteen, and the twenty-five stone movers and builders left the village, and Ord sat in the sunshine with Mud Face.

"Why are you so big?" Mud Face asked.

He smiled. "I don't know. There are many things I don't understand. A man is usually big if he has a big father."

It began to rain, and they moved under the shelter that protected the fire from the rain. "There are lots of things that I'd like to understand," he said. "I'd like to know why it rains. When it doesn't rain, the crops die. If we understood how rain works, we could make it rain."

"People offer sacrifices to the gods to make it rain," Mud Face said.

He leaned towards her so that no one could hear what he was saying. "As you know, I don't believe in sacrifices to the gods anymore. They've never worked. People who are ill make sacrifices, but they still die. For several years, we had very little rain in the summer, and hundreds of sacrifices were made to the gods, but it still didn't rain. This year there's plenty of rain. It will either rain or it won't, and it doesn't matter what we do."

"I think you're right," she said. "But what about the healing stones? Aren't they supposed to heal people and animals? Do they work?"

"I don't think so. People carry bits of a healing stone around with them, but they still become ill and die. Have you ever seen the Hill of the Gods?"

"No. I've heard about it. Have you seen it?"

"Yes."

"What's it like?"

"The Hill of the Gods (Silbury Hill) is very big," he said.

"Do people still carry dirt to the top?" she asked.

"Yes. It was once the burial mound of a great man, and people believed that putting dirt on his grave would make them stronger and cure their illnesses. The grave eventually became a hill. I went there with an old man who wanted his illness cured. He had a bad leg, so I carried his possessions for him."

"Did he get cured?" Mud Face asked.

"No. He carried, or should I say, dragged, two baskets of dirt to the top of the hill, but it was a waste of time. It didn't cure him, and he died a few days later. When I was at the Hill of the Gods, I saw an old woman dragging a basket of dirt to the top. She said that she was in terrible pain. I offered to help her carry her basket, but she said that she had to do it; otherwise, she would not be cured."

"Was she cured?"

"No. She died on the top of the hill and rolled all the way down to the bottom."

Mud Face frowned. "Doesn't anything cure you if you're ill?"

"I don't think so. I think you either get better or die."

"If you don't believe in the power of the gods, why are you building the Home of the Gods?" she whispered.

"To keep the people happy and to give them something to do. Vistern was right when he said that people are weak and need something to believe in. People are happier if they think that the gods are protecting them."

"Do you believe in any gods?" she asked.

"I don't know. There must be some gods somewhere, I suppose. I just believe in the spirits of our ancestors."

"Do we need to sacrifice to these spirits?" she asked.

"Why would we sacrifice to the spirits?" he asked.

"The spirits might help us if we did."

He took a long drink of beer. "I don't think the spirits have any power. I don't think they can help us or harm us. If they could harm us, I would be dead."

"Why?" she asked.

"I've killed many men, and they must hate me, and their spirits would harm me if they could."

"I wonder where we go when we die?" she asked.

"I don't know any more than I know where we were before we were born."

"I feel very confused," she said.

He stood up and looked up at the sky. The moon, as well as the sun, was in the sky. "I think the moon's got lost. It's supposed to be the god of the night. Shall I mock the gods?"

She stood up and held his arm. "No."

"Why not? I did it before, and nothing happened."

"Something might happen this time. I've tried to convince myself that the gods do not exist, but they still worry me."

"You should stop worrying," he said. "Vistern mocked the sun god, but nothing happened to him."

"It did," she said. "He died."

"Only because I killed him. I challenged the gods because I had to know if they were real. I'm now totally convinced that they are just objects and do not have any power." He stood up and looked about to make sure that he was not being watched and that no one was near enough to hear what he was saying, and he raised his hands into the air. "I don't believe in you sun god or in you moon god. And I don't believe in the god of health and fertility."

He waited, but nothing happened. He put his hands down. "If the gods had any power, they would have struck me dead."

"The gods still frighten me," she said.

"Come on," he said. "Let's go to the Home of the Gods."

She stood up. "Am I going with you?"

"Yes. I want you with me at all times. I will always take my gold and you with me wherever I go. I can't afford to lose either of you."

"Are we riding there?" she asked.

He stared at her. "Of course we are. If we have horses, why should we walk?"

"I thought you had mated the horses," she said. "Will it harm the foals if we ride them?"

"No. According to Fillan, it will not harm them to be ridden. The gestation period of a horse is almost a full year. The foals will arrive during the next summer."

Mud Face, Ord and his four bodyguards rode off to the Home of the Gods with Dip running on ahead. It was only a short distance from his village. The light rain stopped, and the sun came out. They arrived and climbed off their horses. Ord inspected the holes that had been dug to house the god stones. From what he could see by looking at the plan of the Home of the Gods, they looked to be in the right places.

They sat on one of the healing stones that were lying on the ground and began to eat the food they had brought with them.

"What's so special about this place, Ord?" Gorda asked.

"I don't know," Ord said. "It's supposed to be a holy place."

"What makes this place a holy place?" Gorda asked.

"According to the wise men, it's because of that," Ord said, and he pointed.

His four guards and Mud Face stood up and looked to where he was pointing.

"What are you pointing at?" Mud Face asked.

"The roadway that leads up to the Home of the Gods," Ord said. "The roadway was not made by men. It's supposed to have been made by the gods and points to the holy ground and to the midwinter sunset."

They all sat down again.

"What's going to be built here?" Fillan asked.

Ord handed him the plan of the Home of the Gods, which was drawn on a hide. "According to the wise men, this was just a henge at first, with just a circular ditch and mound. They then erected wooden god posts and put up a circle of healing stones."

Mud Face looked at the large healing stone she was sitting on. "How did they get these large stones here? Did they drag them?"

"No. Large stones are too heavy to be dragged. They rolled them in the same way they roll all large stones by putting a circle of wood around each end. The wood acts as wheels, and it is then easy to move them."

"Where did they get the healing stones from?" Gorda asked.

"According to the wise old men, a powerful leader in the distant past gathered up all the healing stones he could find and brought them here. The healing stones are very hard and different to the other stones."

Fillan, who had been looking at the plan, said, "The Home of the Gods will be different to all other stone temples. No other stone temple has stones on the top of stones."

"There will be five stone temples for our five gods in the centre of the circle," Ord said. "Each temple will have two walls and a roof. The five temples will be surrounded by a circle of healing stones and then by a circle of temples for the guards of the gods. Each guard will have his own house."

"How long will it take to build?" Hindern asked.

"I don't know," Ord said. "It'll probably take ten or more years, but it will last forever when it is built."

"I know how they roll the large stones," Fillan said. "I've seen them do it. What I would like to know is how they get the large stone to stand upright and go into the hole?"

"They make a ramp of earth next to the hole where the large stone will go," Ord said. "They then roll the stone to the top of the ramp and then take the earth away from the end of the stone that is nearest to the hole, and the stone slides down into the hole."

Mud Face looked at the plan. "The stones that will be the roofs of the temples of the five gods and for the guards of the gods are even larger than the healing stones. How are you going to get them on top of the huge god stones and the guard stones?"

"Ord pointed to the plan. "When all the large stones have been erected, dirt will be put inside the circle and around the stones, and they will make a long ramp made of dirt. The men will then roll the roof stones up the ramp and into position. When the roof stones have been erected, the earth will be removed. It was all planned and designed by wise men many years ago."

"How do you know all these things, Ord?" Fillan asked.

"By listening to the stories told by the wise men," Ord said. "At first, holy places were just henges or burial grounds or where people were cremated. People then began to erect god posts on these holy places, and then god stones. According to the wise men, it's taken over a hundred years to prepare all the stones for the Home of the Gods. All we have to do now is to erect them."

*

Over the next few days, Ord began to worry about how long it was going to take to build the Home of the Gods. The wise men had told him that with only twenty-five men to work and move the stones, it would take about fifteen years. They now had eighty men working and moving the stones, but it was still going to take seven or eight years. Ord sat down by the fire and opened the map of his land.

Fillan sat down next to him. "What are you looking at, Ord?"

"The building of the Home of the Gods is going to take at least seven years," Ord said. "I don't want to wait that long to see it built. We need more men to work and move the stones."

"Then get each village to give more men," Fillan said.

"It will be difficult for the villages to supply more men and to supply them with the food they will need," Ord said. He pointed to the map. "I think I'll incorporate these three tribes into our tribe. It'll give us about a hundred and fifty more men to help build Home of the Gods."

"When are we going to attack these other tribes?" Fillan asked.

"As soon as I assembled my army of fighting men," Ord said. He pointed to the map. "We will attack this tribe to our west first."

*

With an army of over two hundred fighting men and dressed as a high priest, Ord paid the leader of the tribe to the west of his tribe a visit. Ord's men surrounded the leader's village at dawn, and Ord rode into the village with his bodyguards, followed by his men. "Who is the leader of the tribe?" Ord shouted.

"An old man walked towards him. "I am."

"What's your name?" Ord asked.

"My name's Driss. What do you want?"

"I'm the leader of the two tribes to your east," Ord said. "You have a choice to accept me as your leader or die."

"I will not accept you as my leader," Driss said. "We'll fight if we have to. I've heard all about you, Ord. You're the new high priest. We'll accept you as the high priest, but we will not kneel before you."

Ord, who was still sitting on his horse, looked about. Driss had over fifty fighting men with him, and each man had an arrow to his bow. Even though Ord would win if a fight started, he would lose many of his men. "You have many fighting men with you, Driss. You were obviously expecting me. Let me explain the situation. I'm the only one who can talk to the gods. The gods have ordered me to build the Home of the Gods. They have also ordered me to kill you if you do not accept me as your leader."

"Then you will have to kill me," Driss said.

Ord was pleased to see fear on the faces of Driss's men. "Then I will kill you." Ord looked about. "I will also kill every single man who fights me today. If you put down your bows, you will live."

"My men will fight," Driss shouted.

"I want everyone to watch what happens," Ord shouted. He put his sword in its sheath and moved his quiver so that he would be able to use an arrow. "I want you to watch the gods kill your leader."

Driss and his men looked about nervously.

In the blink of an eye, Ord pulled an arrow out of the quiver and shot Driss in the throat. His movements were so quick that Driss's men were taken by surprise, and they did not shoot their arrows. As Driss writhed about on the ground in agony, Ord shouted, "Get on your knees."

Without hesitating, Driss's men threw down their bows and knelt on one knee. Ord raised his bow in the air. "I am the high priest. I am invincible."

The men stood up, and everyone began shouting," Ord is invincible."

The shouted praise eventually stopped, and Ord sat down by the fire with the elders of the tribe and explained what he wanted them to do.

"So, you're allowing us to choose a new leader of the tribe?" one of them asked.

"Yes," Ord said. "I'll expect an annual payment from you, and I want a man from each village to help build the Home of the Gods. I will want at least twenty men."

An elder pointed to a strong-looking man who was standing by the fire. "We'll want Sang to be the leader of the tribe."

"Come here, Sang," Ord said.

Sang walked towards him and knelt on one knee. "I accept you as my leader."

"Good," Ord said. "Sit down by the fire and eat with me."

They began to eat and drink beer.

"Will we be able to keep our gold, Ord?" Sang asked.

"Yes. You'll also be able to have horses. Just make sure I get fifty men to help build the Home of the Gods."

"I will," Sang said.

Ord returned to his village feeling very pleased with himself. He decided to rest for a few days before visiting the other two tribes.

*

Five days later, the leaders of the two tribes Ord intended to incorporate into his tribe paid him a visit. They both knelt before him.

"Why are you here?" Ord asked.

"We've been told that you intend to attack our tribes and join them with yours," one of them said.

"That is correct," Ord said.

"We're here to tell you that we both accept you as the high priest and as our leader and will be sending you men from each of our tribes to help you build the Home of the Gods."

"Good," Ord said. "Sit down by the fire and eat."

*

It was the end of another long day. Ord, Mud Face and Dip were standing just outside their village, watching the sun sink below the hills. The sky was as red as blood, and the moon was already in the sky.

"The sun and the moon gods are watching us," he said.

"I thought you didn't believe they were gods?" she asked.

"I don't. I was joking. They're just objects and cannot think, see or hear. I don't know what they are, but they are not alive. What are you doing?"

"I'm holding your hand," she said.

"Why?"

"I wanted to. How much do you like me?"

"A lot."

"You love meat and beer," she said. "Do you love me like you love meat and beer?"

"That's a strange thing to ask," he said. "Why do you want to know?"

"I just do. I love you more than I love meat and beer."

"You do?"

"Yes. Do you love me like you love meat and beer?"

He looked at the sunset. He did love her like he loved meat and beer, and he would be lost without her. "I also love you more than I love meat and beer."

She squeezed his hand and looked up at him. "I'm pretty I am." She was pulling her funny face and speaking like a simpleton.

He looked down at her and smiled. When she pulled her funny face, she looked ugly. "You're not. You're ugly."

"I'm not ugly," she said. She was still pulling her funny face. "I'm pretty I am."

They began to laugh, and their laughter echoed across their land.

Printed in Dunstable, United Kingdom

77567533R00080